THE TASTE OF LOVE

Book of Love, Book Three

Meara Platt

DRAGONBLADE PUBLISHING, INC.

Additional Dragonblade books by Author, Meara Platt

The Book of Love Series
The Look of Love
The Touch of Love
The Taste of Love

Dark Gardens Series
Garden of Shadows
Garden of Light
Garden of Dragons
Garden of Destiny

The Farthingale Series
If You Wished For Me (A Novella)

*** Please visit Dragonblade's website for a full list of books and authors. Sign up for Dragonblade's blog for sneak peeks, interviews, and more: ***
www.dragonbladepublishing.com

To all who are romantic at heart

CHAPTER ONE

Wellesford, England
September 1815

"BOLLOCKS," THADDIUS MACLAUREN, Laird of Caithness, muttered the moment he spied young Phillip Sherbourne running from the lush, green copse of trees beside Sherbourne pond toward the manor house, his laughter so gleeful, it could only bode ill for his latest victim.

Thad handed his mount to one of the waiting grooms and hurried to the entrance of the house in time to catch the boy at the door. "Pip, what's in your hand?"

It looked like a woman's gown, and since the boy had just come from the direction of the pond, from the very spot where one went to undress before jumping in to swim naked in the water… "Och, lad. Ye didn't. Is it Loopy's?"

A guilty look swept over Pip's face. He tossed the white muslin dotted with embroidered pink flowers at Thad, and with a muttered "uh, oh" took off into the house.

Thad stared at the soft fabric in his hands, exhaling a moan as his fingers began to tingle. Seems Penelope Sherbourne did not have to be in the gown for his body to respond. Just knowing it was hers, taking in her familiar wild strawberries scent was enough to get his heart pounding.

He hadn't seen Penelope since her brother's wedding to Poppy

Farthingale a fortnight ago, purposely avoiding her now that The Book of Love had come into her possession. She had yet to use a single 'recipe' out of this mysterious book on him, but it did not seem to matter. He already had the urge *to mate with this fertile female* as the author had described in explaining the science of a man's brain.

He needed to get his hands on the book, for he'd received warnings about it from his friends, Alexander Beastling and Nathaniel Sherbourne, and wanted to be prepared to combat whatever scheme Penelope was plotting to use on him.

Alex was the Duke of Hartford and known as Beast to his friends. He had been taken down first by Penelope's friend, Olivia Gosling. A fearsome Beast bested by a Little Goose. Nathaniel, the Earl of Welles, had fallen next and married Poppy Farthingale. Was it a coincidence that his two friends had lost their hearts to Penelope's best friends?

And now Penelope had possession of The Book of Love. What did it bode for him?

He glanced up at the sun as it beat down on him from a cloudless, blue sky.

Sherbourne Manor was usually a bustling hive of activity, but no one other than a few stable boys, a footman at the front door, and a gardener seemed to be about, for it was shortly after noontime, the hottest part of the day, and no one would be strolling about the grounds unless required, as these men were, for work.

Sighing, he ran a hand raggedly across the nape of his neck and started toward the pond, the fabric still in his tingling hand and the summer sun beating down on his head. He strode down the path toward the copse of trees and the pond where Penelope was swimming in all her natural glory.

He wasn't going to delegate the chore of handing back her clothes to anyone but himself. The girl was too beautiful, and no man could be trusted. Other than him, of course.

He wasn't going to peek.

Not that he was particularly honorable or a gentleman, and even though Loopy was the most maddening woman in existence who deserved an occasional set down, he was not about to humiliate her by ogling her in the altogether without her permission.

He would look his fill if she ever allowed it, but that was never going to happen.

To her, he was just a big, arrogant Scot with an irreverent attitude and a smart mouth. "Loopy," he called out, stopping at the edge of the trees and overgrown hedges along the pond. "Don't come out of the water."

"No, Thad!"

He stepped into the copse, ducking under branches laden with green leaves and nudging aside honey-scented hedgerows. "Stay in the water. I'm going to place your gown on the branch of–"

His heart burst, for there she stood at the very spot he'd warned her not to be, her auburn hair long and wet and curling about her breasts and hips. "Bollocks, I told ye–"

Her banshee shriek almost ruptured his eardrums. "Don't look! You big, Scottish oaf! I'm not..." She shrieked again and grabbed the gown out of his hands.

He finished the sentence for her in his mind. *Not dressed. I'm not dressed.*

"Mother in heaven!" She was practically naked except for the wet chemise she'd worn to swim that hid nothing from his view.

Nothing.

Not the rosy tips of her breasts.

Not the ample roundness of those breasts. Nor the blessed curves of her exquisite body and her long, shapely legs.

He closed his eyes and turned around, his mouth hitting a jutting tree branch in his haste to blindly step away. "Damn it, Loopy! I warned ye not to come out of the water."

"I was already out, you dolt. You marched in like an invading Hun and gave me no time to jump back in."

"Ye could have alerted me to that fact," he muttered testily, for his heart was still in a rampant roar and he'd now cut his lip on the protruding branch.

"I said *No, Thad*. Was that not enough of a clue?"

"I thought ye were agreeing with me. As in, *No, Thad. I will do as ye say for once in my blessed life and not come out of the water.*" He put a finger on the spot of the cut and felt the warm ooze of blood. "Figures, I'm back less than five minutes and already bloodied because of you."

"You're hurt?" He heard a momentary rustling, no doubt Loopy hastily tossing off her chemise and donning her gown before she came up to him, her manner now gentle because she was a soft-hearted Harpy and could not bear to see him hurt.

He opened his eyes and studied her as she began to fuss over him. This is why he could never dislike her no matter how much she vexed him. She thought of him as a big, dumb Scot. But he was *her* big, dumb Scot, and he'd never known kinder treatment from anyone whenever she sensed he needed it.

"Oh, Thad," she said in a breathy moan, running her thumb lightly over the spot to wipe away the small trickle of blood. Her wet chemise was dangling over her arm, so she took it and raised the gossamer fabric to his mouth to use it as a cloth. "I'm so sorry. Does it hurt?"

"No, Loopy. I'm fine."

She shook her head and laughed. "I wish I could say the same for myself. But it's all my fault, isn't it? I trusted Pip to behave. I ought to have known better. Where is that devil-child anyway?"

"He ran inside the house." Thad couldn't resist brushing a stray, damp lock of her hair off her cheek and tucking it behind her ear.

She smiled at him. "You must be tired and hungry. How was the ride from Plymouth? Any news on your regiment?"

He tried to stifle his ache, but Loopy knew him better than anyone alive and sensed it immediately. "I'm so sorry, Thad. I know how weighing these weeks of delay have been on you. I'll have Cook make up a batch of your favorite scones. They'll be ready by the time you finish unpacking and wash up."

"Thank ye, Loopy."

A pink blush spread across her cheeks. "I don't suppose I can ask you to forget what you saw just now."

He nodded. "Of course. Done."

Her eyes rounded in surprise, relief shining in those dark emerald orbs. "Really?"

Lord, how could a smart-mouthed girl still be so gullible? "No, lass. I will remember the wild tumble of your hair and the sight of your naked body into my dotage. It is burned into my brain. Once seen, it can never be unseen."

Her blush deepened and spread to the tips of her ears and down her neck. "I was not naked. I had on my chemise."

"Which covered absolutely nothing."

She gasped, and then looking quite pained, began to nibble her lip in obvious dismay. "Promise me you'll never speak of it to anyone."

"Aye, Loopy. That I can promise. Ye need have no fear o' that."

He brushed back another stray lock of her hair, for the wind had suddenly picked up and now carried a hint of cool air to signal the end of summer. Since she'd donned nothing but her gown and did not have a stitch on beneath it, he could see she was responding to the sudden coolness. Goose bumps appeared on her arms. Her lips began to tremble when another gust surrounded them.

His gaze drifted lower.

Aye, the lass would put him into an early grave.

"Thank you, Thad." She dabbed at his lips again. "I think the bleeding has stopped."

But his ache hadn't.

What was he going to do about this girl? She was Nathaniel's sister and raised to be a consort to a prince or other elevated nobleman. He was just the laird of a small clan in the upper tip of the Highlands. His lands were as far away from the glittering London ballrooms as any rugged patch of hills and crags could be and still be considered a part of this sceptered isle.

Sheep outnumbered men by the thousands.

Winter lasted almost nine months out of the year.

"Thad, are you coming in?" She was now poised at the door and eyeing him with concern.

He gave a curt nod. "Aye, lass."

"But one more thing." She took a deep breath, then blocked the doorway. He could have lifted her out of the way had he wished, for she was a little thing despite her big spirit that could bring a full-sized man to his knees. "I've made a decision."

"Ye have?"

She shook her head. "One I don't think you'll like."

He arched an eyebrow in expectation. "Just say it, Loopy."

"I've decided to use you as my test frog, after all." She tipped her chin up in the stubbornly defiant manner she always used when she was in the wrong but wanted to do what she wanted anyway.

"No. We discussed this before I left for Plymouth." He frowned at her, his gaze steady in response to her penetrating stubbornness. "Ye will no' be dissecting me. I will no' change my mind about it, so save your breath."

"It may be so, but I've given it considerable thought, and you're the only man I can trust for these delicate experiments."

"Spells."

"What?"

"They're spells or recipes or whatever else you wish to call them, but they are not experiments. There's nothing scientific about attracting a man."

"There is so, and The Book of Love proves it. So, it's going to be you for my test frog. It has to be you."

6

"And once again, the answer is no."

She remained in the doorway, her arm across it to bar him from entering. "These experiments can be dangerous, as Olivia and Poppy have pointed out to me, and I won't put myself in harm's way with a stranger."

"There's a simple solution. Destroy the book."

She stiffened her spine and cast him that stubborn look again, one he knew well from all the years of their acquaintance. "Are you mad? No. I will protect it with my life."

He shrugged. "That's your privilege, but I'll have no part of it."

"Of course you will. Meet me in the garden in an hour. I'll have tea and your favorite scones set out for you."

"No."

"Raisin scones."

"No."

"Hot and fresh from the oven."

He crossed his arms over his chest. "Have them sent up to my quarters."

She mimicked his stance. "You'll find them in the garden. Where I'll be. With the book."

He cast her a wicked grin. "Ye shouldn't do that, Loopy."

"Do what?"

"Fold your arms beneath your–"

"You big, dumb Scot!" She raised her hand to swat him on the shoulder, but he caught her hand in his own and lightly drew it toward his lips to kiss her knuckles. She cast him her fiercest frown as she wrenched her hand away. "In the garden. Or I'll come after you with Cook's rolling pin."

He threw his hands up in surrender. "Ye would, too. Wouldn't ye? Och, ye're a bloodthirsty lass."

She nodded. "So what's it to be? Rolling pin to the head or hot, delicious raisin scones?"

He lifted her up by the waist and easily moved her out of the doorway so she no longer blocked his path. Her body was soft and warm. It took all the determination he could muster to release her. "Scones it is."

But if he wanted to be honest with himself-which he didn't-the only hot and delicious thing he desired was Loopy.

Would he have the strength to resist her?

He needed to get his hands on The Book of Love and find out how to defend himself against her experiments. Lord, help him!

What was she going to do to him?

CHAPTER TWO

AFTER SEEKING OUT Mrs. Plunkett, the Sherbourne cook, in the kitchen and requesting scones for Thad, Penelope hurried upstairs to her bedchamber to change her gown.

"M'lady, has something happened?" her maid asked, pausing in her task of airing out the sturdier gowns she would be needing with the onset of autumn.

"Yes." She began to tell Emily all that had happened. "First, my cousin steals my clothes while we are swimming."

"That imp!" Emily shook her head and sighed, the blonde curls peeking out from her mob cap, bobbing. She was slightly older than Penelope, a pretty girl with a plump, full figure that men obviously found attractive, because she had beaus by the buckets while Penelope had not a single one.

"He left me stranded in nothing but my wet chemise." She held it up to Emily who quickly took it from her hand and set it aside for cleaning.

"Oh, goodness! So, you had to run back here without your clothes?"

"Well, no." She glanced down at the gown she was wearing, albeit with nothing underneath. "As you can see, I did get my gown back."

"Lucky thing!"

Emily was genuinely sweet and not very clever, but none of her young men seemed to mind. Penelope wasn't certain what she did when she went 'out' with each beau, only that they kept coming back for more. "M'mum warned me never to go swimming with men. Young master Phillip is just a boy, but they start early, m'mum said."

Penelope sighed. "Apparently, they do."

"He's a sweet lad when he wants to be. At least he returned your clothes and all is well now."

"He did no such thing."

Emily scratched her head as she regarded her. "But you're wearing your gown. He must have given it back."

"Laird Caithness returned it to me."

"Lud! He's here?" Emily's eyes widened in delight and then she burst into giggles. "I wouldn't have put my clothes back on for him. Oh, lud. Him I would have dragged into the water with me for a…swim."

"Emily!" Despite having a sweet and sunny disposition, she also had an earthy nature when it came to men and pleasure.

"Sorry, m'lady." She glanced down at her toes and stopped giggling. "I know it's very different for ladies of your noble rank. So much as an innocent kiss might ruin you. To be honest, I'm glad I'm not you. I like kissing men."

Penelope knew she ought to put an end to this inappropriate conversation, but she didn't. "I've never kissed a man."

"Never?" Emily's gaze turned sharp and assessing, and she slowly grinned. "That big Scot would do it proper."

Yes, and she was determined to have Thad kiss her. Not right away, of course. There were other tests to perform on him before she got to the more dangerous ones. But she did plan for him to give her a test kiss. How else was she to compare his to the 'right' kiss from a man she could love?

Thad was not that man.

How could he ever be the right husband for her?

He was raw and untamed. He teased her mercilessly. He was irreverent, impertinent, and arrogant. He would never be a biddable husband. Not that she wanted a doting milksop, but shouldn't there be something other than the two of them constantly butting heads? Besides, his home was in Caithness. It may as well have been on the other side of the world; it was so isolated and foreign to her.

A young woman would have to love Thad to the depths of her soul to give up London and the lovely Cotswolds and all her friends and family to… What was she thinking? Thad would return to Caithness as soon as the ship transporting his regiment arrived in Plymouth. He'd ride off with his brothers, cousins, and others of his clan, and she'd likely never see him again.

The thought saddened her.

She wasn't certain why, for they hadn't seen each other in years until this summer. She'd known him when she was a little girl. He, Beast, and her brother, Nathaniel, had been schoolmates. Beast and Thad had often come to the Sherbourne home for holidays or casual visits, especially Thad, for he lived too far north to make it to his home and back in the few weeks between end of term and start of another.

"But will he stop at just one kiss?" Emily asked, nudging her out of her musings. She began to giggle again, one of those knowing, naughty giggles.

"What?"

"Would you want him stop at just one? I would clutch that big body of his and–"

"Emily, enough!" Did the girl have no common sense? "I am not going to kiss him. Certainly not right away. Perhaps never. Most likely never."

Her maid shrugged and began to rummage through Penelope's wardrobe for proper undergarments and a new gown for her to wear. "What about this apricot dimity? It's just the thing."

Penelope nodded. "It'll do nicely."

The gown was more sophisticated than her day gowns, the neckline fashionably styled to accentuate her bodice. Modestly, of course. The London fashions were more daring, but here in the countryside, one did not walk around with one's assets spilling out.

The aroma of raisin scones wafted into the hall as she descended the stairs and made her way to the garden. Soames, their ever-reliable butler, had set out cups and plates on one of the wrought iron tables under a shade tree and would soon wheel out the tea cart.

She was just about to sit down when she spotted her friends, Olivia and Poppy, walking toward her. "We're going to Miss Billings's bookshop for this week's reading club," Olivia said. "Care to join us?"

"I can't. Thad is back."

Poppy gasped. "He is? When did he return? More important, what are you going to do to him?"

"Nothing." She reached for The Book of Love she'd brought down with her. "Well, something obviously. But this book is about love. I'm not putting him through the twelve labors of Hercules."

"Go easy on him," Poppy warned. "Nathaniel says he's going through a difficult time now that he's home and his regiment has been delayed over a month returning to England. And he's received no lists yet. That cannot bode well."

Olivia nodded. "Beast says the same. He's worried about Thad. But perhaps these tests are just the distraction he needs. We'll help you, of course."

"Olivia is more of an expert than I am." Poppy shook her head. "I don't know what I did to your brother to make him fall in love with me. I'm just glad he did. And the best part... Well, one of the best parts," she continued with a blush, "is that we are now sisters. And Olivia is our closest neighbor. We'll always be together."

Olivia cleared her throat. "Not if Penelope marries Thad. He'll take her back to his home in the Highlands."

"Which is why I have no intention of marrying him." Penelope needed to put a stop to any matchmaking plans her own friends would hatch. "This is why he's safe. I've decided to set my cap for the Earl of Wycke. He seems to be a very nice man. His mother and sister are lovely. His seat is within a day's ride of Sherbourne Manor."

Poppy nodded. "And he's nice looking, too."

"Yes, I suppose he is." Penelope shook her head with more conviction. "He is."

Olivia frowned. "Well, that was a rousing commendation of him. Does the mere look of him raise butterflies in your stomach? Curl your toes?"

Penelope stifled her frustration. "Not yet, but I intend to work on falling in love with him once we're back in London. I'll see how Thad responds to my various tests and then use the same ones on Wycke. Simple enough."

Both of her friends looked doubtful, but they said no more as Thad appeared. They greeted him warmly and then marched off to Wellesford, whispering to each other and giggling as they hurried away.

"Where are they going?" Thad had washed and shaved, and changed out of his dust-stained travel clothes into finer garments. He now wore buff breeches, a white lawn shirt that enhanced the breadth of his chest, and a vest of deep, forest green that seemed to bring out the hazel-green of his eyes and the dark, chestnut red of his hair.

"Miss Billings has started a reading club. They've become members."

"Ah. And you?"

He wore no cravat or jacket, which was typical of him not to conform to proper attire, but she couldn't berate him for it. The air was warm and moist, and the breeze that had earlier felt cool upon her skin because her clothes were wet, now felt hot and made her fresh gown stick to her body. Autumn would soon be upon them, but it was still uncomfortably warm. Or was it Thad's nearness that was kindling her insides? He looked awfully big and ruggedly handsome. How could

:rlook his muscles when he refused to cover them up with a
jacket.

"Me? I've joined the book club as well, but I'll skip this meeting
since you're back and we have work to do."

"Ye are doing nothing to me until I have my raisin scones." He
sank into the chair beside hers and stretched his long legs in front of
him.

His boots were scuffed from wear, but she did not pass a comment. Nathaniel's valet, Greville, would attend to it later. "Here they
are now," she said when Soames brought out a platter of divinely
scented, piping-hot treats along with the tea cart. "A dozen for us to
share."

He arched an eyebrow and grinned. "What makes ye think I'm
sharing them?"

She laughed. "Very well, hoard them for all I care. My gowns are
too snug anyway, what with all these weddings to celebrate and me
testing every course of the festive food before it was set out."

His expression turned wicked. "Snug looks good on you. No man
will complain about that." He nodded to the tome bound in faded red
leather on the table beside her. "What does your book have to say on
the subject?"

"Do you wish to start our work now?" She was pleasantly surprised, certain he'd give her endless trouble even about reading a mere
page or two. "I thought you'd prefer to eat first."

He leaned close. She tried not to grow giddy from his divine scent
of musk and maleness. Oh, she'd read The Book of Love several times
over and understood the importance of the five senses. Touch. Taste.
Sight. Hearing. Scent.

Her senses were in a mad spin right now, trying to take all of him
in. *His look.* Splendid, of course. He was big and hard-muscled, and had
a handsome face. Not in any elegant, classical sense, but still strikingly
appealing. *His scent.* It took all her resolve not to throw her arms

around him and put her nose to his neck to breathe him in. Animals used scent to attract each other, and apparently civilized beings did as well. She doubted Thad was purposely using his scent to attract her, for she was the last woman on earth he wished to entice. He thought of her as a pesky gnat he could not swat away.

Still, she took a few more breaths of him.

Discreetly, of course.

"I can work and eat at the same time." He frowned. "Or don't ye think this big, dumb Scot can handle two tasks at once?"

She frowned back. "Don't say that about yourself." She cast him a sheepish grin. "Only I can say it about you. And you know I don't really mean it. However, you are thick-headed and impossibly annoying at times."

"Och, lass. So are ye," he said in a soft, teasing way so that his brogue slid over her like warm honey. Oh, the *sound* of his voice! She'd always liked its deep, rumbling lilt.

She sighed. "I know. But you must admit, you purposely instigate. No one else riles me as efficiently as you do. You have only to cast me *that* look and I start squawking like a mad hen."

He appeared surprised, even a little confused. "What look?"

"Any look," she admitted. "Even a mere glance will set me off. There's always a challenge in your eyes. We never simply engage in conversation. We spar like boxers in a match, each one trying to land a blow to the other."

He frowned. "Loopy, how can ye think I'd ever hurt you?"

"Never intentionally. I know you love us all. Me, Olivia, and Poppy, as though we were your sisters."

"I do, lass. Ye know I'd give my life to protect any of you."

"I know." She realized he had yet to touch a scone, so she lifted the platter to offer him one. He grabbed three, for he could fit no more on his small plate. This is what she liked about him, the zeal with which he approached everything. Always grabbing the fistful, never holding back. But it was hard to keep up with him at times.

He took a big bite of his scone and moaned in pleasure. "I'd marry Mrs. Plunkett if she weren't already taken. These taste like heaven."

Penelope laughed. "Oh, Thad. Your secret is out. The way to your heart is through your stomach."

"Aye, lass. I won't deny it." He polished off the first and started on another. "Food of the gods. That woman is a treasure. If your brother weren't my best friend, I'd steal her from him without a moment's remorse. My cook at Thurso is a wicked old viper by the name of Fiona. She boils the flavor out of everything. Ye can crack a tooth on one of her biscuits."

"Oh, you poor boy. I can see how it has stunted your growth."

He laughed. "Fortunately, my uncle sent me off to boarding school when I was a scrawny lad of six. Everyone complained about the meals, but compared to Fiona's cooking, what came out of the school kitchens was, in my opinion, manna from heaven."

Her heart gave a little tug, recalling what her brother had told her about Thad's childhood. He'd never known his mother. She'd died giving birth to him. His father had died shortly afterward, leaving him and his older brother in the care of one of their prominent family members, the Earl of Caithness, a granduncle of theirs.

To her dismay, she realized she knew little else. He'd been the youngest, raised with his older cousins and an older half-brother, then sent off to boarding school. Only six years old at the time. Too young for a boy to be separated from his loved ones.

Pip, the little devil, was two years older than Thad had been when sent off. She couldn't imagine Pip not being with them, not getting hugged or tucked in at bedtime.

What had Thad been like as a boy?

How could she have been so thoughtless, never asking about his early years or his family situation?

"Loopy, why are you staring at me?"

"Am I?" She gave a casual laugh that sounded forced even to her own ears. "I hadn't noticed."

He grinned. "Lass, just come out with whatever it is ye're thinking. Ye know I'll get it out of ye sooner or later."

"It isn't anything awful." She sighed and shook her head. "In all the years you've joined us for holidays and term recesses, I never once thought to ask about your family. I simply thought of you as one of ours. How–"

"Don't." Pain etched his features. "Don't ask now."

"Why not?" She'd responded on impulse and realized too late that mentioning his brother and cousins was hurtful. They were part of the regimental ship, the one already a month overdue. He was mad with worry about them, the concern festering like a raw and gaping wound to his heart. "I'm so sorry. You don't have to answer the question. Ignore it. Ignore me."

She stuck the platter out to him once more. "Scones?"

"Aye, Loopy." He grabbed another three and stuck them on his plate. But he didn't eat them, just stared at them for a long moment. "It's the delay," he said in a ragged whisper. "The longer it goes on, the more I fear they'll return in coffins."

She placed her hand on his arm, feeling as though she'd placed her hand on solid rock, for he was tense. "The war's over. I pray it is merely a matter of logistics, of the burden of bringing home so many soldiers all at once. You Scots are a stubborn lot. Far too stubborn to come to harm. I'm sure it is nothing more than official complexities causing the delay."

He ran a hand through his hair that was a little too long and curling at the nape of his neck. "It's disease I'm worried about. Men in close quarters under bad conditions."

"Scots are also a hardy lot. You're raised on oats and that awful haggis. Your stomachs are cast iron."

He chuckled.

She tossed him a gentle smile.

He caught it and held it for an endless moment, gazing at her in a way that melted her insides. Thad? Melting her bones? Firing her blood? Impossible.

She looked away. "Care for some tea?"

He nodded, picking up one of the untouched scones on his plate and quickly washing it down with the tea. "I appreciate ye trying to cheer me, Loopy. But these wartime diseases are something awful. They can fell a man faster than a musket ball or a bayonet." He turned to study her once again, but this time he was unsmiling. "This is not a conversation for us to be having. Tell me what ye've been doing since Nathaniel and Poppy's wedding."

"Nothing particularly important or significant. Reading The Book of Love, of course." She cast him a wry grin. "Trying to keep Pip out of mischief. An impossible task, by the way. Entertaining the occasional gentleman caller."

He arched an eyebrow in surprise. "You have a beau?"

She felt a sudden heat to her cheeks and silently berated herself for blushing. "I wouldn't quite call either of them that."

Now he appeared genuinely surprised. "More than one?"

"Two gentlemen have paid me a visit since Nathaniel and Poppy's wedding. Can you believe it? The Earl of Wycke and his sister stopped by a few days ago. And one of Nathaniel's London friends, Lord Jameson, came around as well. Do you remember him? He joined us the same weekend Charlotte and her father were here."

"So did Wycke," Thad remarked.

She gave a mock shudder. "Good riddance to the duke and his daughter. Thank goodness Nathaniel regained his sanity in time."

Thad set down his scone. "What do ye think of him?"

"Lord Jameson?" She scrunched her nose to mark her distaste. "I can't take him seriously. He's looking for an heiress and nothing more. His gaze is too assessing, his manner too fawning. He told me I was beautiful. He mentioned it repeatedly, as though trying to convince himself more than me."

Thad listened with interest. "Loopy, I know I give ye a hard time. But ye are a decent-looking lass. If ye weren't always scowling at me, I might tell ye the same."

"What, that I'm beautiful?" She shook her head and laughed. "I think I'd suffer an attack of the vapors if you ever said anything that hinted of being a compliment."

He let out a genuinely lighthearted chuckle that rumbled deep within his chest. "Tell me more about Wycke."

She shrugged. "There isn't much to say. He's a gentleman. His sister is very nice, too. He doesn't leer or ogle me, so that's in his favor."

"Do ye like him, Loopy?"

She glanced at The Book of Love. "Yes, of course I do. He's quite pleasant."

"That's a rousing affirmation."

She frowned at him. "Well, what am I supposed to say? We've chatted little more than once or twice. I don't know him very well. It's too soon to feel one way or the other about him. But I am inclined to think favorably of him." She tipped her chin up, awaiting Thad's challenge.

She'd set her cap for Wycke. So what if there was no heat or aching passion between them yet? It signified nothing since she'd had no experience with passion and wouldn't know what it felt like anyway. But this was her plan, to learn about it with someone safe. Namely, Thad. "Perhaps I'll marry him. Assuming he asks me, of course."

Thad nodded. "A most sensible answer. Are ye judging a baking contest at the Wellesford annual fair, because it doesn't sound like ye're speaking of a potential husband. Inclined to think favorably? Does he make your heart skip beats? Does he sweep ye off your feet?" He made an irritating scoffing sound. "I speak with more passion about these raisin scones. Probably about my oatmeal porridge, too."

She leaped at the opening he'd given her. "Precisely my point. This is why I need you to teach me. How am I supposed to know about feelings for a man when I've had no experience? And who better to guide me than you? My brother trusts you. I trust you, even though you're an annoying bee sting to my backside most days. The point is, I'm safe with you. We are not in love, so we are unlikely to do something stupid with each other. No improperly wanton urges to worry about."

He choked on his tea.

"Are you all right?" She slapped him lightly on the back.

Goodness, he was big and muscled everywhere.

"I'm fine." He nodded, but he was still coughing and his eyes were turning red and tearing. He took another sip of his tea as he struggled to calm his breaths. "I am not going to do anything improper with you."

"Isn't this what I just said? It's perfect. I'll never have a moment's worry as we explore the sensations that are supposed to enhance our connections to form deep and abiding bonds of love." She reached for the book and opened it to the first chapter. "Love does not come from the heart but from the brain. It is the brain that sends signals throughout the body, telling you what to feel. Therefore, to stimulate a man's arousal—"

Thad put his big paw across her hand. "Skip that part. Yer brother and Beast told me all about the male's lower brain function."

"We can't skip it. This is what defines a man, the compelling need to mate with any female he deems fertile in order to spread his seed far and wide." She pursed her lips and frowned. "I need to see your low brain function at work."

"It's always at work." He arched an eyebrow and cast her an irritating smirk. "I'm male, aren't I?"

Indeed, he was.

Big and handsome and strong. Protective, too. Which had to explain the sudden tingle of recognition coursing through her body. Women had urges of their own, the book explained. She was eager to learn more about those. But the male urge was to sow his seed far and wide. However, not just any woman would do. His low brain made a quick assessment of every woman he encountered. Those deemed too old, too young, too sickly, were quickly dismissed.

Those deemed fertile became the desired object of his attention.

The female urge was to find the mate who would protect her and her children, to choose the mate who would stay close to their home and fight off predators. Because if he abandoned her and their children, they would be left defenseless and eaten by wolves.

She cleared her throat.

He was looking at her, waiting for her to say something more. "Thad…"

"Don't ask me again, Loopy. We're done with this conversation."

He still had his hand over hers. It felt warm and delicious. The pulse at the base of her throat spiked suddenly. She couldn't make it stop. "Now that's cleared up. *Ahem.* Yes, nothing more to be said on the topic. Let's move on to the five senses."

She slipped her hand out of his and set the book aside a moment because she had one more question to ask him on the subject of his lower brain function. She hoped he would be honest about it. The answer was important to her. "Thad."

He groaned. "No, Loopy."

"But it's at the heart of the matter. What do you see when you look at me? My…" She glanced down at her bosom before returning her gaze to his. "My…*those* attributes… Would you consider me a desirable female? And if so, what is it about me that you find desirable?"

He was giving her that look again, the one where he appeared not to be breathing. "Pass me another scone."

She grabbed the platter and held it out of his reach. "Not until you answer my question. What do you see in me that makes me desirable?"

"It doesn't matter what I think. It's Wycke you have to convince."

"But you're my test frog, and I have to know how you respond. Just be honest. It is only the physical attributes I'm interested in for now. I understand it signifies little beyond your low brain acceptance of me. Forget our years of friendship. And our years of butting heads. If you were seeing me for the very first time, what would your low brain assessment be of me?"

"Loopy, stop fishing for compliments."

"I'm not. We are speaking of science, not romance."

"Then scientifically speaking..." He stared at her for what felt like an endless moment. "Och, lass," he said with a soft ache to his voice. "Ye're a most desirable female. An attractive vessel for any man's seed."

"Including yours?"

He groaned again, this time adding a roll of his eyes to mark his exasperation. "Ye'd be more desirable if ye passed me one of those scones ye're cruelly holding out of my reach."

She stuffed one into his open mouth. "Why are you always so difficult? I only needed a yes or no."

He took a bite of the scone before setting it aside. "Then it must be a no."

"It must?" She didn't know why she felt so disappointed. She'd always found him to be extremely handsome even when he irritated her, which he did almost all the time. She just assumed that he'd found her equally appealing. "Oh, I see."

She supposed it was safer if he had no feelings for her.

Still, it hurt.

Her eyes began to water, so she quickly turned away to blink back the tears now welling at their corners and threatening to spill onto her cheeks. Good heavens! He couldn't ever see her cry over him.

He sighed. "Bollocks, Loopy. Of course, ye're beautiful. Of course, I'd be mad for ye if we were meeting for the very first time. What man wouldn't be?"

He took her hand and wrapped it in his. "How are we going to get through these tests if ye cry at every response?"

"I'm not crying, you big, Scottish oaf."

"Ye're breaking my heart, lass." He ran his thumb across her cheek to rub away the moisture, but quickly drew it away once the task was accomplished.

"I am?" She hastily dabbed at another stray tear before turning to him.

He nodded. "I'd do anything not to see ye sad."

"Then you'll help me?" She smiled when he emitted a light moan to signal his agreement. "Truly? But you must always be honest, even if it hurts my feelings. Honesty is most important. Shall we try again?"

He shot her a look that warned it was a big mistake, so she braced herself for the answer she feared would be hurtful to her pride. But honesty was all that mattered. Besides, it would reinforce her argument that she was safe with Thad. He was never going to be swept up in wanton feelings for her or ache to hold her in his arms.

"Och, lass. Honesty?" He raked a hand through his hair and his gaze turned surprisingly hot and smoldering. "If I saw ye for the very first time?" His voice was a gentle rumble. "I'd think I was looking upon an angel."

Her eyes widened and the breath caught in her throat.

"But my wicked brain would quickly take over. I'd be looking at yer breasts and finding their fullness to my liking. Then I'd be looking at the rest of yer fine body and finding it equally pleasing. I'd be looking at yer lips and wanting to kiss them, wanting to feel their softness against my mouth. I'd want to wrap ye in my arms and have my way with ye."

Fertile female. Need to mate with her. Those were the words used in The Book of Love, but Thad was speaking to her in his deep, honeyed brogue, making her insides melt. On his lips, the words did not sound scientific at all, just deliciously seductive.

Penelope cleared her throat and broke away from his torrid gaze. "The book describes the male brain as functioning on two levels, the low and the high. When a man's brain is at its lowest functioning level, he is only thinking of sex. But it is a necessary function, for this is how he spreads his seed and populates the earth with his offspring."

She turned to him, saw his gaze was still hot enough to melt her insides, and quickly glanced at the book again. "This is the importance of the question I asked you. What do you see when you look at me? By your description, I think you would find me to be a suitably fertile female."

She felt his grin, but refused to look up. "I think your assessment is that I'd be among the women with whom you'd choose to mate."

He gave a choking laugh. "Loopy! I know ye don't think much of me, but I'm no hound. Among the women with whom I'd mate? There'll only be one for me. That'll be my wife. And I'll be marrying her as soon as I return to Caithness."

"You have a sweetheart? In the Highlands?" Her heart sank straight down to her toes. When would he have met her since he'd been away fighting on the Continent all these years? Perhaps an arranged marriage to a girl he hardly knew. "I didn't realize. Will you marry her before the year is out?"

"Lass, what business is it of yours? Why should you care?" His expression sobered. "But it's time. Beast is now married. So is yer brother. We'd thought to have a little fun when we got home. Sow a few more wild oats. In truth, our hearts weren't in it."

Penelope held back a sigh of despair. Thad with a sweetheart? It wasn't fair of her to resent it, but she wasn't ready to share him with anyone else just yet.

"England is finally at peace, lass. Who knows for how long? What we three quickly realized we needed, despite our bravado, was the love of a good woman. Someone to hold in our arms each night. Someone to bear our bairns and make us a family."

He placed his hand over hers. "Ye needn't worry. Beast found his Goose. Nathaniel found his Poppy. But I know we are not meant to be. So, I'll help ye with Wycke, but ye must be honest with yourself. Don't force yer heart to feel something it cannot feel for him or ye'll be unhappy for the rest of yer life."

She merely nodded, too overcome to speak without her voice shaking.

Why was he suddenly so wise and tender?

Had he always been this way, and she'd just never bothered to notice? "Thad, promise me you'll do the same. Don't settle for just anyone. She must be perfect. Kind and gentle, and genuinely caring for you."

He regarded her as though she'd suddenly grown two heads.

But she was undaunted. "Promise me, Thad. *Please.*"

Who was this girl?

Tears threatened to fall again, but she fought them back. Why was she suddenly so overset he'd found someone to love?

Could it be because it wasn't her?

CHAPTER THREE

"**W**HAT ARE YE going on about, Loopy? Why should ye care if I have a sweetheart or not?" Thad muttered, wishing Pip would come along and drop a spider in their midst to break up their conversation. "Ye've already said ye have no wish to marry me."

"I don't." But she had her chin tipped up in indignation and was casting him a fiery look that would burn a lesser man to cinders.

"Then my love life is irrelevant." He didn't have one anyway. No sweetheart. No mistress. No casual dalliances. Just an ache in his heart for this fiery, sharp-tongued girl who would never have him. "So let's get on with this test frog business. Read me the chapter about the five senses."

Not that he wanted to continue, but he didn't have the strength to break away. Where was that devil-child when one needed him?

And where were his friends? Nathaniel should have noticed his arrival and joined them by now. Sherbourne Manor was his home, after all. Beast was often in London these days, so it was possible he'd left Goose behind at Gosling Hall while he ran around on official Crown business.

"Each sense has its own chapter," she said, breaking into his thoughts and regaining his attention. "Shall we start with the sense of sight?"

"Whatever you suggest." He glanced around. "And speaking of sight, I haven't seen Nathaniel yet. Where is he?"

"He and Beast rode to Coventry early this morning, but they'll be back in time for supper."

"And where is Lavinia? I'm sorry, lass. I should have asked earlier." Stumbling across Loopy in nothing but a wet chemise still had his senses in a wild tumble. The incident had occurred over an hour ago, but his body had yet to cool down.

Hah.

His blood was on fire, and if the blasted girl refused to stop talking about physical attributes and shoving The Book of Love at him, he was going to behave like a low brain specimen and do something very, very foolish.

And now they were to speak about the sense of sight. What more could he say?

Although he'd described the look of her when discussing his low brain sensibilities, his opinion would not change as they moved on to the higher functions of the male brain. She was the prettiest girl he'd ever met, and she grew prettier by the day. The sight of her filled his heart with joy even when she vexed him.

He would keep the thought buried deep inside of him.

She did not want to hear those words from him.

Penelope began to nibble her lip. "My aunt hasn't been feeling well lately. I hope it's just a passing discomfort, but I'm worried about her. That nasty business with Andrew Gordon seems to have overset her. She hasn't been quite herself ever since. Nothing I do or say seems to help."

She cast him another vulnerable look.

Twice in one day.

He rarely saw such a look on her face, for she was a determined force of nature and never appealed to anyone for help.

"Thad, I can understand Nathaniel being angry about the bounder forging his signature and pretending to act on his behalf while up to no good. But why would my aunt still care so greatly? I think something more happened, but Nathaniel won't tell me, and neither will Lavinia. Has he said anything to you?"

"No, lass. But I haven't pressed him on the matter. He'll tell me if he wishes to."

Penelope pursed her lips, a mark of her displeasure. "How can we leave it alone? It could be something important."

"It could. But it's none of our business until Nathaniel decides to make it our business." He thumped his hand on the book to hold it at the page she had opened. "Read the chapter about the sense of sight. I'm curious what it says."

She sighed. "I'll never understand men."

He arched an eyebrow. "And I'll never understand women."

"I suppose this is why The Book of Love is so helpful. It educates us about our differences, but also about what we have in common." Her lips remained pursed, but she said nothing more about the Andrew Gordon affair.

After a moment, she removed his hand from the page and looked up at him again. "The author claims what we overlook is as important as what we see. I think a good test would be for us to look at each other and discuss what we notice about one other. Hold nothing back."

"Ye're asking for my opinion again? This time thinking about what I've missed." He leaned toward her and a slow grin spread across his face. "I'll have to study ye closely. Now that's an intriguing proposition. I'm to use you as *my* test frog."

Her eyes rounded in horror and she gasped. "No, you are not to test anything out on me. This is merely a preliminary discussion."

"Ah, I see. Ye're scouting me out. Ye've decided it helps to know what the enemy is thinking."

He didn't mean it to be hurtful, but she took it that way.

She cast him yet another pained look. "You are not my enemy. This isn't a battle. This book is about the beauty of love and how our happiness as a couple is enriched when we use our five senses. Not that you and I are a couple, or ever will be."

"I know, lass. I meant nothing by it. I've spent most of these past eight years in the midst of war. One campaign after another. My brain hasn't settled to peacetime yet."

"Oh, Thad." She rested her hand on his arm again. "I'm so sorry."

"No, lass. Don't be. I survived with hardly a scratch on me. And I'm here now, among friends." He playfully tugged on her ear. "Yes, I consider you a friend. Even though ye're still the most vexing lass I've ever met. Now, do as the book says. Look at me. What do you see?"

To his surprise, she blushed to her roots.

Hell, what did she see?

He stifled a grin as he noticed the pulse at the base of her neck begin to throb. Her tongue darted out to moisten her lips. Thad was no coxcomb, but he knew the signs of a woman interested in a man. Loopy would fly off like a Harpy if he dared mention it. There was no point. Mere physical attraction was not enough to convince Loopy to marry him. "I see a big man. Handsome in a rugged way. Broad mouth. High cheekbones. Wicked glint in your eyes. Your turn."

"I've already described you physically."

She glanced at the pages again. "Describe my other attributes. What do you think of when you look at me?"

"Trouble." He leaned even closer and grinned. "But a good sort of trouble, if that makes any sense. You're opinionated. Always challenging. Ye think for yourself. Nothing bland or docile about ye, lass. Ye'll never be a biddable wife to any man."

He ran a hand through his mane of red hair. "Ye may be a Sassenach, but ye have the heart of a Highlander. I mean it as a compliment."

He wasn't certain how Loopy would take his words, but was not about to find out. Pip chose that moment to burst out of the house and tear across the garden toward the back gate leading onto the road to

Wellesford. His implacable governess, a sturdy Scotswoman by the name of Addie, ran after him. But the boy was young and spry, and Addie, who looked to be about forty years old, would never catch up to him.

"Bollocks, what did the lad do now?" He rose, and Loopy did the same. "I'll go after him."

"I'll go with you," she said.

"The lad is obviously overset. Stay here. Let me talk to him."

She frowned. "Because he'll respond better to a man?"

"Yes." This is what he meant about her not being docile or biddable. If he said night, she'd say day. If he said no, she'd say yes. Besides being vexing, she was the most contrary lass he'd ever met.

Arguing with her was useless. And now Pip was almost at the gate and about to run onto the road.

He took off after the lad, quickly passing Addie who was breathing hard and had her hand clutched to her rib cage. He caught the boy and snatched him up in his arms. "Whoa, Pip. Where are ye going?"

"I don't want to take a nap!" He squirmed in Thad's arms.

Addie and Loopy caught up to him. "Och, the rascal deserves to be sent to his room without his supper," Addie said between deep gulps of air. "The little bandit tipped over his mattress and said he wanted to see the horses."

"There's a yearling sale in town today," Loopy confirmed. "Pip's gentle mare is quite old and frail." She said nothing more, but her expression was all he needed to see to understand her concern. The lad had lost both parents. She didn't want him riding an aged mare who could very well die while he was in the saddle.

"Nathaniel said I could have my own horse when I'm older." Pip was still squirming, but Thad wasn't letting go of him. "I want a horse. I want a real horse!"

Perhaps the fear of another beloved thing dying was what sparked Pip's tantrum. Although they teasingly referred to Pip as the devil-child, the lad also had a lot of good in him. Thad hoped his mischief would be tempered by maturity as he grew into a man. "I'll strike a bargain with ye."

The boy quieted and regarded him steadily. "Are you tricking me?"

"No. I'd never lie to ye." He set the lad down but kept a hand firmly on his shoulder to keep him from taking flight again. "Addie, it's all right. I'll take him into town to see the horses. Pip, I'll let Nathaniel know if I see any good prospects." He cast Pip a warning glance. "But only if ye behave. If ye run off, the bargain's off. And ye must abide by Nathaniel's opinion when he returns."

Pip nodded and grabbed his hand. "Let's go. Let's go! The best horses will be gone if we're late."

Thad laughed, but allowed himself to be drawn along.

Loopy joined them. "I'll go with you."

Addie waved them off with a gentle caution. "Ye behave yerself, young Master Pip, or ye'll be answering to me."

Thad was relieved for the distraction, although having Loopy by his side, laughing and chatting with Pip as they walked into Welles-ford, did not give him all that much relief. Her auburn curls were fashionably styled atop her head, but the locks were thick and satiny, and he ached to unpin the lush strands and watch them cascade down her back in splendid waves.

He wanted to run his fingers through her hair.

He wanted to do unmentionable things to her.

He supposed this was his low brain working extra duty, for he could not stop looking at her as a wolf might look upon a juicy rabbit. He liked the sway of her hips, the graceful tip of her head as she smiled up at him. The fullness of her breasts, of course.

Stop looking at her that way, idiot.

She took his arm as they approached the town square where the horse pens were set up. Mostly men were milling about, for this was not considered a suitable venue for females. However, no one was going to chase away the sister of the Earl of Welles.

Loopy's excitement was palpable, and so was Pip's.

The boy squealed with delight when Thad lifted him onto his shoulders. "I'm a giant! I can touch the sky!"

Loopy's laughter was as sweet as morning dew. "Oh, Pip. Stop bouncing up and down on Thad's shoulders. He isn't your horse."

They watched while a few yearlings were auctioned off, then melted away from the crowd and proceeded to walk among the livestock awaiting their turn at auction. Thad was riding before he could walk, so he knew more about good bloodstock than any man in attendance, including any acknowledged experts.

He'd spent the war years in the Royal Scots Greys, to his way of thinking, the finest dragoon regiment in the king's army. A good dragoon was one with his horse, for his life depended on the beast while in the heat of battle. "This one looks interesting," he said, running his hand along the withers of a handsome gray. Let me speak to the owner."

Pip cheered.

Thad cast him a warning look. "No promises, Pip. This horse may go up for auction today. But since the horse fair runs for another few days, I'll see if the owner will hold off selling him until tomorrow. Nathaniel and Beast will be back this evening, right?"

Loopy nodded and began to run her hand up and down the horse's nose. "He is a nice-looking colt. Sweet disposition, too."

Thad could see Pip was struggling to contain his excitement. "He's the best," the boy said with a squeal. "I'm going to name him Monarch."

"If Nathaniel approves." Thad patted the lad's shoulder. "Go have a lemonade with Loopy while I talk to the owner." He turned to her. "I'll meet you at the Golden Hart once I'm finished."

She nodded and went off with the lad who wasn't walking so much as bounding and leaping for joy.

He watched them leave, unable to take his gaze off her until she disappeared from view. Wellesford, the Cotswolds, or a glittering London ballroom is where she was meant to be. He had to keep reminding himself of this, for these little moments had him thinking they might have a chance at love.

He shook out of the thought.

She'd never leave her life behind just for him.

And what could he offer her?

After speaking to the owner and getting him to agree to wait until tomorrow to put the gray colt up for auction, he went to the Golden Hart to look for the pair. Convincing the owner to hold off wasn't hard to do. The possibility that the Earl of Welles would acquire one of his bloodstock had the man salivating.

Thad found Loopy and Pip seated at one of the wooden tables outside of the Golden Hart enjoying their lemonades. Poppy and Goose had joined them.

Pip leaped up when he saw Thad striding toward them. He picked the boy up and twirled him around. "Can't promise anything, Pip. But he'll hold off selling the colt until tomorrow."

"Monarch! Monarch! Thank you, Thad." The lad gave him a heart-felt hug.

Loopy's eyes were bright and dancing with merriment as she thanked him as well. No hugs, but he preferred it that way. He'd make a fool of himself if she ever fell into his arms.

He'd never have the strength to let her go.

He chided himself again. He had to stop thinking about her and the possibility they'd build a life together. No, he would never be anything but her reluctant test frog. Perhaps he'd get a kiss out of it in the course of her experiments.

That's all he desired.

One kiss would satisfy him.

It would have to satisfy him.

But he knew it wouldn't. No amount of convincing would ever make him believe it. Just one? He wanted to kiss this girl a thousand times and more.

When the ladies finished their lemonade, Poppy and Goose climbed into Goose's waiting carriage. To Thad's surprise, Loopy chose to walk back with him and Pip, even though the wind had picked up. It was a cooler, quite damp wind that threatened rain by this evening. She sidled up to him while Pip ran a little ahead of them down the road. "You were brilliant today, Thad. Thank you for what you did for Pip."

"Nathaniel would have done the same had he been here."

She smiled at him, and despite the gathering clouds, the sun seemed to shine a little brighter. Everything suddenly seemed brighter, no matter that the sun was now lost behind a gray cloud, and even if it hadn't been, they were strolling down the roadway in the shade of the trees.

She smiled at him again.

The world lit up for him once more. The grass seemed a little greener. The wildflowers dotting the surrounding meadows bloomed with uncommon splendor. The stone of the walls lining the roadway shone a deeper, richer Cotswolds gold.

But the most beautiful colors were the auburn of Loopy's hair, the soft apricot of her gown, and the glittering emerald of her eyes.

"Thad, how long will you be with us?"

He arched an eyebrow. "Looking to be rid of me already?"

She chuckled, knowing he was merely teasing her. "No, not this time. You are Pip's hero. You're even a bit heroic to me. But don't get too full of yourself. I'm sure you'll do something to irritate me before the day is through."

She tucked her arm in his. "I was thinking of tomorrow evening's supper. What do you think of mutton and Yorkshire pudding?"

"Loopy, lass, ye know how to entice yer test frog. Ye know it's my favorite."

She shook her head and laughed. "I have you all figured out. The way to your heart is through your stomach. You are ridiculously easy to please. You eat anything and everything. Is there a food that isn't your favorite?"

"Certainly. Ye know I dislike eels."

"Anything else?"

He shook his head. "That's about it."

Pip broke into a run once the manor house came into view. Since Addie was waiting on the garden steps for him, Thad did not feel the need to chase after the lad.

Neither did Loopy.

"So, how long will you be with us this time?" she asked again.

He shrugged. "I don't know. It depends on when I get word of my regiment's arrival in Plymouth. I'll ride back there by the end of the week if I receive no news. I can be of some use organizing the settlement of the arriving troops, even if they aren't my men."

"Is there anything we can do to help?"

"Nathaniel has already offered. We'll rely on your hospitality once my regiment arrives and we start the march north to Caithness. I'd like them to camp here for a few days while I ride to London and meet with Lord Castlereagh. He's been running all over the Continent, but he's due back in town by next week."

Penelope held him back a moment. "Why must you meet with him?"

"I'm the surviving commanding officer, and yet he's kept me here instead of on the Continent with my men. Now, I've heard rumors he plans to keep the Royal Scots Greys in France, those who are healthy enough to serve. So why am I here and not over there with them? I don't like it. Not one bit."

"Perhaps he has something more important planned for you."

"Then why keep me sitting around, doing nothing all this time?"

He gave a sigh of disgust. "After Major-General Ponsonby died in battle, I led our regiment in battle. Now that the war is won, no one has been appointed to replace me. It churns my gut to be apart from them. I need to understand what is going on. I want answers, and not from some officious clerk who wouldn't know the right side of a bayonet if it poked him in the arse. No, I'm going straight to Castle-reagh, and if I canno' find him, then I'll seek out Wellington."

"Is there not a field general or someone else of rank you can turn to instead? Beast, for example."

"I may have to rely on him if I'm not granted an audience with either of them. But I doubt they'll deny me. The Royal Scots Greys are like no other fighting unit. We're the king's finest dragoons." He smiled wryly. "I suppose every regiment makes that claim. In truth, we saw little direct action until Waterloo. We were used primarily as support for the infantry, covering their retreat, securing the land they'd gained. Clearing the enemy nests that remained. Protecting the injured as they were carried back to the hospital ships."

"How was Waterloo different?"

"We were no longer held in reserve, but placed in the thick of battle. My regiment led the cavalry charges. Our objective was to push back the French until they were forced into a disorganized retreat. Ponsonby fell rather early in the battle, so it was left to me to lead the men."

Loopy's eyes were wide as she listened with bated breath while he recounted the details.

He was merely reporting the facts of this final battle, but she looked at him as though he was her hero. He couldn't bear it, so he turned away and continued to walk toward the house. She walked beside him, still holding onto his arm so that he had to slow his pace.

"Thad, we defeated Napoleon. Why does it matter so much to you that you were brought back here? You look so angry?"

"France is still a dangerous place. There's much left to do to restore it to a real and lasting peace. I agree with Castlereagh's desire to keep his light cavalry units on the Continent, at least for now. I hope that's what he'll do. If this turns out to be his plan, I want to be the one leading my men. I can't sit around, twiddling my thumbs while there's important work to be done. If pushed to it, I'll resign the damn commission and go to France on my own."

She cast him a soft smile. "You're a stubborn, prideful Scot. I'm sure it will all work out and you'll stay a dragoon until the last man is brought home."

He shrugged.

Her expression turned thoughtful. "There must be a reason why you were made to return. I know it wasn't a lack in your fighting skills or leadership. Did you anger someone important?"

He shook his head and gave a mirthless laugh. "Not this time. I behaved myself. The lives of my men were at risk. I'd never do anything to harm them, much as I would have liked to strangle more than a few of those idiot generals. No, lass."

He shrugged again. "The only thing that makes sense to me... I suspect the Earl of Caithness made the request."

Her brow furrowed in obvious confusion. "Why would he? You're not his heir."

"Indeed, I'm not. Two cousins and a brother in line before me. However, I think Caithness trusts my judgment more than he does the others." He arched an eyebrow and grinned. "What? Nothing to say, Loopy? Are ye too stunned to speak?"

She laughed. "I always suspected you were smarter than you appear. My brother wouldn't be best friends with an idiot." After a moment, her smile faded. "I'm proud of you, Thad. I'm so proud of the three of you, and relieved you all returned home safely."

He tucked a finger under her chin to draw her gaze to his. "I don't know how safe I am while you're in possession of that book about love. But I suppose if I survived Napoleon, I'll survive you."

"Don't make a jest of it," she said and turned away to walk toward the garden instead of the house.

"Bollocks, lass. What has you overset now?" He raked a hand through his hair, wishing he were more adept with women.

He couldn't seem to do anything right around her, for she often confounded him. In his own defense, he had never known a mother's love nor ever had to deal with sisters. Other than Penelope, Olivia, and Poppy, he'd never been around any gentlewomen. His experience had mostly been with harlots, and he wasn't all that experienced, for being with just any woman had never appealed to him.

No, he'd always been the one-woman sort.

Now that he was back, he knew who that one woman would be for him. But he was so wrong for her. He was no silver-tongued rake. No glib flattery or witty words flowed from his lips. He couldn't be in Loopy's presence for more than a few minutes without upsetting her.

He followed her into the garden and sank down beside her on the stone bench in the center of the circle of rose beds. "It isn't anything you said." She spoke in a soft, ragged voice and refused to look at him. "It's merely my own frustration. You've done so much with your life, and what have I done besides living a life of ease?"

"Loopy, ye've kept the Sherbourne household running in Nathaniel's absence. Ye've made a welcoming home for all who visit. Ye care for the wellbeing of the citizens of Wellesford and all those who work for your family. Ye'll do the same for the man ye marry, no matter how large his estate or elevated in rank he is, ye'll handle it all with an easy grace."

"So I'm to be a well-dowered housekeeper?"

Thad groaned. "Och, lass. Why do ye always twist my words? If a man wanted a housekeeper instead of a wife, he'd get himself a housekeeper. A wife is a partner, someone in whom he can confide his innermost thoughts and concerns. And before ye toss back another smart remark, a wife is also more than a convenient bedmate. If a man cared only for sex, he'd know where to buy it."

Blessed saints! He'd been a little too blunt in his speech. He wouldn't blame her if she slapped him. To his surprise, she leaned her head against his shoulder. He wasn't certain what to do, so he put his arm around her. "What if I don't marry? What am I then, Thad?"

"Anything ye want to be." He wanted to tell her that she was the only one holding herself back, but that wasn't true. He understood the restrictions placed on an upper-class spinster. It wasn't merely the men who would ignore her. The women would be even more dismissive, for this is the way Society had set their minds. Unmarried, she would be thought of as a poor relation residing in someone's home. Married, she would be a leader in Society.

Same person. Different status.

Poppy and Olivia would never treat her that way, of course. They were true and loyal friends. But the rest of Society? No, Penelope had to marry.

He sighed, for this discussion of status had him thinking once more of all he lacked. He was a captain in the Royal Scots Greys, but for how long? Would he be sent to France or back to Caithness to serve his granduncle, Earl Caithness.

The earl had given him leadership over one of their small Highland clans. In truth, it was a kind gesture, allowing him the title of Laird Caithness. But it did not alter the fact that Penelope Sherbourne was far above his station.

"Thad, would you ever consider..."

"What, lass?"

She shifted in his arms to face him, her expression one of distress. His heart was ready to rupture with ache for this girl who felt so warm and soft in his arms. Why couldn't it be? What would he lose in asking her? Never mind that he was unsettled. Never mind that he had so little to offer her.

Before she had the chance to finish her question, Thad heard someone approaching. He eased Loopy out of his arms and rose to face whoever was coming toward them.

She rose as well to stand beside him. "Nathaniel," she said with a happy gasp, "how was Coventry?"

"Business went smoothly." He kissed his sister on the cheek and then eyed Thad with curiosity. "I see you've been busy in my absence."

Did he mean with his sister? As in attempting to seduce her? Which was always on his mind but nothing he'd ever act upon. "I–"

"I hadn't taken two steps into the house before Pip accosted me. He's so happy and wouldn't stop chattering with excitement. Thank you for picking out a horse for him. A gray, just like the horses in your regiment. That was well done of you. I'll speak to the owner first thing tomorrow and purchase it for the little devil."

Thad shook his head and laughed. "Ye'll have your hands full with that lad. I'll give him some riding lessons while I'm here. Teach him some simple things."

Nathaniel arched an eyebrow. "What do you consider simple? I don't want him falling off his horse on his first day out."

"No jumps. No galloping. Just a trot around the meadow." He held his hands up in mock surrender. "I promise."

Nathaniel still eyed him warily. "All right, but don't move him along too fast. None of your cavalry tricks."

Loopy tipped her head in curiosity. "What are cavalry tricks?"

"Has Thad never told you?" Nathaniel appeared surprised. "He's one of the finest horsemen in Scotland. And England, in all likelihood."

Her eyes brightened, and she cast him that soft, melting look that made him feel like a hero again…which he was not. He knew a few tricks on horseback. That was all.

"Show me, Thad. Please."

He scowled at Nathaniel but reluctantly nodded. "Meet me in the meadow at sunrise tomorrow morning. That's when I give Thor his workout. I don't want Pip watching or he'll attempt to do the same before he's ready. The lad will break his neck."

She nodded. "I'll be there."

"Poppy and I will, too," Nathaniel said, then cast Thad a wicked grin. "Unless we find something better to do."

"Ugh, Nathaniel!" Loopy rolled her eyes. "You're my brother. Poppy is my best friend." She cast him a look of indignation, and with a huff, turned to Thad. "I refuse to listen to my brother lust after my best friend."

"She's his wife now. He loves her. Isn't that how marriage is supposed to be?"

She laughed and shook her head. "Don't you dare be reasonable about this."

He couldn't help his inane grin in response. "Och, was that a compliment? I never thought I'd live to see the day."

"It wasn't a compliment, merely a statement of fact." But she was smiling at him, and her smile was achingly sweet. "When you're done showing me your tricks, we're going to work on The Book of Love. You're not going to distract me from my purpose."

She huffed again, a magnificent release of air that was regal and imperious, yet innocently charming in a way that only Loopy could pull off.

"Sorry, Thad. I shouldn't have set her off." Nathaniel patted him on the shoulder as they both stood watching her march away. "That Book of Love business. It's nonsense."

And yet, Nathaniel and Beast were now married.

It wouldn't be the same for him.

How soon before his regimental ship arrived? He couldn't wait to get out of here. The thought of Loopy in love with another man was ripping his heart apart.

And he, like the big, dumb Scottish fool that he was, had agreed to help her.

"Thad," Nathaniel said with an unexpected wariness in his tone, "just remember, she's my sister. No matter what ridiculous love demands she tosses at you…keep your hands off her."

"I'll never do anything to harm her, ye ought to know that. It's yer sister ye need to be talking to."

Nathaniel shook his head and laughed. "Tell Loopy something she doesn't wish to hear? I'll never hear the end of it. She'll plague me into my dotage, and will still be railing at me as they lower me into my grave."

"She isn't so bad. Aye, she can be a Harpy at times, but only when she passionately believes in something." After all, she'd been right about Poppy being perfect for Nathaniel. Had she not cared and acted upon it, her brother might now be married to the wrong woman.

Nathaniel frowned. "Am I hearing right? You're defending her? She kicks you worse than she kicks any of us?"

"Usually, I deserve it. She's also kinder to me than anyone alive."

"My sister?" The notion appeared to genuinely surprise her brother. "She tortures you."

He shot Nathaniel a warning glower before turning to walk away. He needed to clear his mind of Loopy and this conversation wasn't helping.

"Blessed saints! Are you in love with Penelope?"

CHAPTER FOUR

P ENELOPE SLEPT ON the window seat in her bedchamber, her curtains open so she did not miss the sunrise. Perhaps it was foolish, but she knew her time with Thad was short, and she refused to waste a precious moment of it.

Yes, she was greedy to have more of this man, to share experiences and build memories to treasure once he walked out of her life, never to return again.

She awoke with an ache in her heart, but refused to allow sadness to get the better of her. So, she smiled as the sun's warming rays fell across her face. Tossing off her covers, she hastily washed and donned a simple morning gown. She put on her walking boots, laced them up, and quietly hurried out of the house.

A moment later, she saw Thad walking his magnificent steed from the stable toward the meadow. "Good morning," she said, a little breathless as she joined him, for the mere sight of him had set her heart fluttering.

He looked as strong and magnificent as his beast.

He was dressed casually, his shirt and breeches molded to his muscled torso. His boots had not been polished yet and were the worn leather of a man used to hard work.

"Morning, Loopy." He cast her an endearing grin and tugged lightly on her braid, for she hadn't taken the time to do up her hair properly. In her rush, she'd simply brushed it back and fashioned it into a loose braid. "I wasn't sure ye'd come to watch me."

"Wouldn't miss it. I stopped in the kitchen and left word for Cook to prepare something special for you for breakfast." She grinned when his expression turned wary. "Special in a good way. Eggs. Sausage. Kippers. Oat cakes, of course."

He nodded. "You're doing it on purpose."

She eyed him innocently. "Doing what?"

"Hitting me at my weak spot. The *taste* of love. Isn't it one of the five senses mentioned in your book?" He held up at the edge of the meadow, firming his grip on the reins as Thor neighed with impatience and pawed the ground, eager to be set free to run. "Ye're working on the scent of love, too." He leaned forward and nuzzled her neck. "Ye smell delicious, just like a sausage patty."

She smacked him on the shoulder. "It's lavender soap, you wretch! I don't smell like a side of pork. And if I do, it's only because I was in the kitchen trying to do something nice for you."

He laughed and tweaked her chin. "Still so easy to rile. Gad, how can ye be so fierce and yet so gullible?"

"Don't start on me, Thad. The sun's hardly up, and you're already irritating me."

He swung himself up on the saddle with an easy grace. "Step back, lass. Don't want ye trampled by Thor. He's friskier than usual today. No doubt, he knows we're going to show off our skills. He's even more arrogant than I am, if that's possible."

She laughed in exasperation, for Thad had a way about him that was as loveable as it was annoying. She could never stay angry with him for long. "Be careful."

She moved back to the edge of the meadow, still in a position to have an unobstructed view of his performance. "Don't run over any deer. They'll be foraging among the hedgerows at this time of the morning."

"I'll stay clear of them." He nodded and gave Thor the slightest nudge. The horse took off with dazzling speed across the meadow. After racing from one end to the other, Thad turned his mount again and slowed him down just the littlest bit. "Watch this," he called out to her.

Suddenly, he slid off the saddle and then hopped back on, and then did it again. All the while, Thor never broke stride. But Thad didn't stay seated in his saddle for long. In the next moment, he leaned low and came up with a handful of wildflowers.

He slowed Thor to a trot and rode toward her. "For you, Loopy." He handed her the small bouquet with an exaggerated showman's bow.

Before she could thank him, he was off again, horse and rider moving as one. Spinning. Leaping. Thad shifting forward, arching back, once even standing on his saddle and tossing her a casual wave as Thor loped past her.

She would have broken her neck had she attempted any of those tricks. But she now understood why he'd survived Waterloo without a scratch. He was a constantly shifting target, able to slip on and off, bend low and disappear from sight, turn suddenly and charge.

He was reckless and fearless.

Her heart was in her throat the entire time he paraded and preened in front of her. He made it look so easy, but she knew the incredible strength required to perform such feats. That's what he was, big and muscled and confident.

He approached her again, but this time, Thor was moving at a breakneck gallop. To her relief, she merely felt a soft *whoosh* as horse and rider tore past her. The scent of horse and saddle leather mingled with the gust of air.

After another turn around the meadow, Thad guided Thor at a lazy trot toward her. She meant to berate him for some of those reckless tricks, but all thought of doing so slipped from her mind as he dismounted in one smooth motion, picked her up, and twirled her in his arms. "What did ye think, lass?" He was like a little boy, hopeful and earnest and so proud of his accomplishments.

But everything about him warned he was no tame, little boy. His body was magnificent, as though sculpted from stone. His arms were pillars of granite. His brow was beaded in sweat and his shirt which stretched from taut, broad shoulder to taut, broad shoulder, was damp from exertion.

In truth, she couldn't think at all. She wanted to toss her arms around his neck and kiss him with abandon. But what if he didn't feel the same and was embarrassed by her kiss?

Worse, what if he did feel the same? She wasn't moving to the Highlands, and he wasn't settling in England. Perhaps, if circumstances were different…but they simply were not meant to be. She tried to shove out of his arms. "Let go of me, you big oaf. Now I'm covered in your sweat."

He laughed and twirled her again. "Ye still smell as sweet as a sausage patty."

She wanted to scold him.

And wanted to hold him.

Mostly, she wanted to be someone important to him, not just a fertile female his low brain determined was a suitable vessel in which to spill his seed. She wanted to be the one woman he'd protect from the wolves who would eat her and her offspring if left on their own.

But he would leave her and ride north any day now.

"Come on, Loopy. Answer me. What did ye think?"

She laughed softly. "You were wonderful, Thad. Wherever did you learn to ride like that?"

He shrugged, but did not release her. She was surprised. However, she said nothing. How could she admit she liked the rough warmth of his hands on her waist? His hands were big and powerful like the rest of him, but he held her quite gently.

She leaned her head against his shoulder, no longer attempting to resist. "Did someone teach you?"

"My brother did, a little." His arms remained around her like a warming blanket. "Mostly, I learned on my own. There wasn't much else to do in Thurso other than herd sheep, which I hated doing," he said, his voice a soothing murmur. "So, I rode out on my own whenever I could. No one missed me."

"Surely, someone did."

"No, Loopy. The men had no patience caring for a boy, and there were hardly any women around to attend to the chore. The few who hadn't left for Edinburgh or distant shores were old and ornery like my cook, Fiona."

"Thurso, is that where you'll settle?"

"Aye, I'm laird there. But I won't be returning immediately. If Castlereagh doesn't ship me back to France, I'll report to the Earl of Caithness. He has a rather fine castle just north of Inverness. Lots to do there. He'll keep me busy."

She arched an eyebrow, expecting that his granduncle had more in mind for Thad than mere chores. He'd likely arrange a marriage for him. It wouldn't take much doing since every woman in Caithness, whether young, old, sweet, or sour, would fall in love with this handsome Scot. Thad had already hinted at having a sweetheart.

It eased her heart, in truth. She and Thad were not meant for each other, but she knew he would find someone lovely to marry once he was ready to settle down.

She tipped her head up to meet his gaze.

The look in his eyes was dark and hungry. The nearness of their bodies excited her. He dipped his head ever so slightly, the subtle gesture seeming to compel her lips closer to his. Yes, she simply had to kiss him before he left. As her maid said, the big Scot would know how to do it proper.

"Loopy…" He spoke her name in a reverent whisper, half groan and half awe. His eyes were fixed on her and his gaze smoldering as he stared back at her. There was a slight downward tilt to the corners of his eyes that gave them a seductive quality, an I-want-to-bed-you look that no woman could resist.

Did he wish to bed her?

No, it was too ridiculous to contemplate.

But he wanted to kiss her…she hoped he wanted to kiss her.

Their breaths mingled.

Her eyes fluttered closed.

But the kiss never came. Thad suddenly drew away. In the next moment, she heard Pip's excited voice. "Thad! Thad! Teach me those tricks!"

"Oh, bollocks." Thad groaned and ran a hand through his hair. "The boy must have been watching from his window."

Penelope loved her young cousin even when he was at his most evil. But right now, she wanted to throttle him. Couldn't he have waited another five minutes before joining them? She turned to Pip with a frown. "No tricks, it's too dangerous. Thad has been riding for decades. You've yet to have a single lesson. I want your promise that you won't attempt anything foolish. You have to learn the basics first. And you have to build up your muscles. It takes great strength to leap on and off one's mount while it's moving. More than you possess right now."

She glanced at herself. "More than I will ever have."

But Thad…dear heaven. *The sense of touch.* Oh, she did enjoy touching that hard, warrior body of his.

Suddenly alarmed by how easily Thad was able to overwhelm her senses, she muttered an excuse to return to the house ahead of him and Pip. Neither seemed to particularly mind, so she left the pair chatting about Thad's horse and the simple tricks Thad would teach Pip and his new horse so long as Pip did nothing foolish.

The boy was nodding and vehemently assuring Thad he'd be good as gold.

Penelope knew better.

Pip was still a little boy. Everyone knew little boys were curious, adventurous creatures. Pip's mind was never idle. He was always thinking, usually of harmless things. But there was also a streak of mischief in him. Not wickedly intentioned mischief, just a need to push the boundaries and see how far he could overstep before being hauled back into place.

Thad obviously had that same streak. *Look at me while I jump on and off my horse at full gallop. What, I might break my neck?*

She went straight into the dining room to make certain the breakfast courses were set out on their salvers. To her surprise, her aunt was already seated at the table with Periwinkle, her adorable spaniel, on her lap. "Aunt Lavinia, I'm glad to see you're looking better. I didn't expect you up this early."

"Good morning, my dear." She cast Penelope a cheerful smile. "I heard Pip stomping down the stairs and thought I'd come down as well. I saw a little of the show Thad put on for you." She arched an eyebrow and cast her a wry smile. "He likes you."

Penelope snorted.

"He wouldn't be so keen on impressing you, otherwise."

She sank into the chair beside her aunt. "Do you think so?" The notion did not please her. First of all, she doubted he liked her above all other women. In truth, he probably liked her far less than other women because she constantly vexed him.

Lavinia patted her hand. "He's a fine young man."

"He's a big, Scottish oaf. He constantly teases me."

Her aunt chuckled. "I find his manner charming. He's like a big, wonderful pup, wanting to be noticed and not knowing how else to gain your attention."

Penelope rolled her eyes. "He could try simply talking to me."

"Oh, dear me. No, that isn't Thad. He isn't refined or glib. He isn't one for witty banter. Nor is he the sort to toss casual compliments or flatter a woman unless he feels it to the depths of his soul."

"Nonsense, Aunt Lavinia." Penelope rose to pour herself a cup of tea. It was a task usually done by one of the footmen, but she felt restless and needed to do something to end this conversation. "He isn't sensitive, nor does he have a poetic soul. Oh, don't frown at me. I'm going to use him as my test frog and that's all. He'll return to Caithness soon. Perhaps he'll be ordered back to France to rejoin his regiment."

A little knot formed in the pit of her stomach. France was still a dangerous place. She didn't want Thad to come to any harm. "Even if he does respond to a few of my tests, it will signify nothing. The effect will wear off. He'll ride away and soon forget me. I shall remain right here, where I belong."

Thad and Pip tramped in before Lavinia had the chance to argue with her. Even Periwinkle was tossing her a doubtful look.

She returned to her seat.

Thad settled his large frame in the chair beside hers and tugged on her braid. "Ye look angry enough to eat Periwinkle. What's the matter, lass?"

He was the matter.

"Och, now ye're tossing me that Harpy look. What have I done?"

Nothing, of course. He was just being himself, and she couldn't stop responding to his nearness. Or stop thinking that perhaps Aunt Lavinia was right. No. Thad could not possibly be the man of her dreams. She certainly wasn't his dream woman.

She was his sausage patty.

Apparently, showing off on horseback aroused a man's appetite. Thad was working on his third helping of eggs when Nathaniel and Poppy joined them a short while later. Pip immediately brightened. "Are we going to see Monarch's owner this morning?" he asked Nathaniel.

"Indeed, we are."

Pip cheered.

Periwinkle's ears perked and his tail began to wag furiously.

Lavinia laughed. "Even dear Periwinkle is excited for you, Pip."

"I'll join you," Poppy said, casting Nathaniel a doting look. "I have some errands to run in town. Olivia's birthday is coming up next week, and Beast asked if we could plan a party for her. He'd like it to be a surprise."

Lavinia clapped her hands. "How lovely. Who will you invite?"

"Our neighbors, of course. Lord and Lady Plimpton. The vicar," she said, referring to the handsome Adam Carstairs. "Dr. Carmichael. Miss Billings. My sister, Violet, will be joining us this weekend, so she'll be here for the party. Lord Lothbridge and his daughters. A few of the town officials."

Penelope sat back and listened as Poppy and Lavinia began to discuss the details, pleased that Poppy had so easily adapted to the role of Nathaniel's countess. Despite Poppy's fears, she was a natural hostess and more than capable of taking on whatever tasks were required of her. She was genuinely kind, and had a calm, soothing manner that put everyone at ease within moments of meeting her.

"Penelope, what do you think?" Poppy asked, obviously wishing to include her in the planning. "Will you review the guestlist and menu with me and Lavinia?"

Penelope smiled and shook her head. "I think the two of you are more than capable of handling this party on your own."

Poppy began to nibble her lip. "But this is your home, too. You and I are both Olivia's best friends. Besides, you've been Nathaniel's hostess here for years."

Penelope reached over and gave Poppy's hand a light squeeze. "And now you'll be filling that role." She grinned. "I'm sure he likes you a lot better than he likes me. I give him headaches."

Poppy laughed. "He adores you."

"I happily leave the party planning to you and Lavinia." She turned to Thad. "Besides, I have a big Scot to tame. He thinks The Book of Love is a joke. I am determined to prove him wrong."

Thad set his fork down on his plate with a clatter. "That damn book. Lass, here's a bit of Scottish wisdom for ye. Give—"

"Spare me your lecture." She rolled her eyes.

He ignored her and continued. "Give a man hearty food, plentiful ale, and a warm bed, and he'll have no reason to stray. Forget the London parties, the fancy balls, and musicales. Forget the fine gowns and jewels, or fashionably-styled hair. Most women look like they've grown a beehive on their heads. Fashionable, my arse. It's all bollocks."

Pip laughed. "Thad said arse! Ha, ha, ha! Arse!"

She frowned at both of them, saving her most scathing look for Thad who was a grown man and ought to have known better than to mouth off in front of the impressionable boy. Why did he always have to be so contrary? "If what you say is true, which it isn't and makes not a shred of sense, then the Season would not be so popular. Lords and ladies would not bring their precious daughters and rakehell sons to London to make advantageous matches. They'd spend no money on fine gowns or entertainments. The modistes and haberdashers would be out of business. The theaters would play to sparse audiences."

"Lass, do ye seriously believe ye need to do yerself up fancy to catch a man's eye?"

She blushed, recalling her state when Thad had first arrived. Hair wet and tumbling loosely to her waist. No clothes to mention other than a wet chemise that scandalously revealed too much. Oh, she'd caught his notice. The wrong sort.

He arched a wicked eyebrow and cast her a devil's smirk to remind her of it.

But it wasn't her fault. She'd been caught unaware by his return. "Yes, one must look one's best when seeking a husband or one will never be noticed amid the crowd."

He shook his head and sighed. "Och, lass. Ye don't belong with those other peahens in the marriage mart."

"Then where do I belong?" She frowned in challenge. Her hands were curled into fists, ready to poke him if he uttered a glib remark.

He shrugged. "I suppose we could study that book to find out."

Which is what she'd planned to do all along. But to get Thad to the point of agreeing with her was as pleasant as having a tooth pulled. She gritted her teeth and cast him an insincere smile. "Excellent. I'll meet you by the pond in an hour."

He chuckled. "Are ye sure ye'd like to meet there, lass?"

She rose, tipping her chin up in that imperious manner she'd perfected as a little girl and improved upon now that she was a grown woman. Well, she was hardly that. But she was old enough to be placed on the market for marriage and that counted for something.

The 'Penelope' look was daunting to everyone. Even her brother ducked when she tossed a fiery glance his way.

But not Thad.

No, she was a game to him, and the big oaf seemed to take unreasonable delight in thwarting her at every turn. He'd been magnificent not ten minutes ago while riding Thor. Now, he was back to his goading self.

He was still chuckling. Was he going to say something about her almost naked swim?

Yes, he was. She saw it in the wicked glint of his eyes.

And then, he did. "Shall I *dress* for the occasion?"

Pip giggled.

"What's so funny about meeting by the pond?" Poppy asked. "And how must one dress when reading a book?"

Pip opened his mouth.

Oh, no! Her devil-of-a-cousin was not going to humiliate her.

She cast Thad a murderous glance for inciting the lad, noticed his chair was tipped back as he sat with his hands casually propped behind his head. *Lord, forgive me.* She kicked the chair out from under him.

All thought of the pond was quickly dispelled as Thad crashed to the floor, his arms and legs flailing like a turtle caught helplessly on its back. "Och, Loopy!"

She stepped over him as he lay sprawled on the floor. "Poppy, make sure you invite the Earl of Wycke and his family to the party."

Thad sat up.

The big oaf looked hurt. Not physically wounded, but his feelings were hurt.

It was his own fault. He shouldn't have been jesting about their encounter, even if the reference was so obtuse, no one was likely to understand it. Pip couldn't have known what transpired after he'd run off with her gown, but the imp would have said something. Which would have led to Nathaniel asking more questions. Which would have led to trouble.

Thad rubbed his shoulder, then began to rotate it slowly. "Och, ye're a bloodthirsty lass."

"And you're a gossipy, old hen." She sighed and knelt beside him. "Are you injured? I'm so sorry. I shouldn't have…accidentally tripped over your chair."

The lie merited no response, so he wisely gave none. But she heard groans and choked coughs and laughter from the others around the table who knew she'd brought him down on purpose.

She ran her hands lightly across Thad's shoulder to make certain she hadn't caused him to break a bone. He allowed her to touch him, but he wasn't happy.

He had a hot, angry look about him.

Was he going to do something to get even with her?

CHAPTER FIVE

PENELOPE STRODE TO the pond with the determination of a field general on a war campaign. She had The Book of Love tucked under her arm, and now all she needed was her Scottish test frog. After their breakfast incident, she wasn't certain Thad would join her...ever. In truth, if he had any sense at all, he'd be running as far away from her as he could.

Any man with half a brain would, her brother had grumbled, admonishing her for purposely knocking Thad off his chair. No one had believed it was an accident, which it wasn't since she had done it on purpose. But it still hurt her feelings that everyone was so quick to believe the worst in her.

Was she truly that awful?

To her surprise, Thad was seated on the fallen log under the large shade tree, staring out across the water while lost in thought. The sun glinted across the pond, causing the blue water to shimmer and sparkle beneath its intense rays.

Sunlight also filtered through the leaves of the giant oak and shone on Thad's copper hair. She liked the thick waves of his hair, the broad expanse of his shoulders, and the ripple of muscle beneath the white, lawn fabric of his shirt as he turned to acknowledge her with a wincing smile.

He arched an eyebrow and moved over, motioning for her to sit beside him. "Where shall we start, Loopy?"

"I'm not sure."

He hadn't moved that far over, so they were seated closer to each other than was proper, their arms grazing as she shifted the book onto her lap. He'd probably stayed close on purpose, intending to rattle her.

Did he intend to push her off the log?

She wasn't going to give him the satisfaction of admitting her discomfort. She'd rather walk across a bed of nails than ask him to move over. No, he could sit right there and feel her elbow jabs in his ribs.

Oh, what was wrong with her? Hadn't she done enough to him? Thad would never hurt her. So how could she consider hurting him again?

She had been staring at the book, but now turned to Thad. "I'm so sorry about this morning. I panicked. You tossed off that veiled remark about seeing me…" Her voice trailed off and she felt the fiery heat of a blush on her cheeks. "About me in my wet chemise…" Because she was not going to acknowledge how much he'd seen of her.

Lord, he'd seen everything.

She cleared her throat. "Then Pip opened his mouth, about to humiliate me in front of all my family. So I did the first thing that came into my mind."

He said nothing, although she'd paused in the hope he might accept her apology. But he wouldn't even look at her. "Oh, Thad. Please don't stay angry. How is your shoulder?"

"Better, lass." He finally turned to face her. "I'm the one who owes ye the apology. I shouldn't have teased ye like that."

"And I shouldn't have responded like a crazed Harpy. Then we're friends again?" She cast him a hopeful smile.

He nodded. "Always."

"Thank you, Thad."

He nodded again and motioned to the book on her lap. "Shall we get to it?"

"Yes." She let out a rush of air in relief. Losing Thad as a friend would have devastated her. "The book speaks of connections we make with each shared experience." Her shared experiences with him were hardly the stuff of dreams, but she wouldn't make the same mistakes again. He deserved better treatment from her. She'd do her best to show her appreciation of him. "But I hardly know the Earl of Wycke. I haven't gone fishing with him as I have with you. Or waded into the pond looking for tadpoles. Do you remember the summer we collected them and they hopped out of my bucket when I tried to sneak them up to my room? Oh, Father had a fit!"

He gave a deep, resonant chuckle. "I remember, lass."

"You tried to take the blame for it so he wouldn't punish me." She shook her head and cast him a mirthful glance. "You shouldn't have stepped forward to protect me. Father knew you'd never bring those creatures into the house. He would have wagered his earldom it was me, and he would have been right."

Thad was still grinning at her, a wonderfully sentimental and affectionate grin. "He sent you up to your room without supper."

"You were more overset about it than I was. You smuggled food to me." She paused a moment to regard him tenderly. "You even gave up one of your precious raisin scones for me."

"I was afraid ye'd melt away to nothing. Ye were such a skinny, little thing. But ye had big eyes and an even bigger smile." Thad nodded. "It was a beautiful smile. I couldn't bear to see ye punished."

"Even if I deserved it?"

"Och, lass. Ye were mischievous but never wicked. Besides, I was at fault for suggesting we go looking for tadpoles in the first place."

"Oh, but we had such fun. How am I to build this sort of bond with Lord Wycke after only one Season?"

He shrugged. "Ye're set on Wycke then?"

The gesture was casual, with no noticeable pain to the shoulder he had been rubbing earlier. She was relieved she hadn't maimed him permanently. He had lovely shoulders, big and broad. The sort a girl could lean her head upon.

And if he wrapped his arms around her...oh, her heart skipped beats.

Although she would never admit it to Thad, there was something quite magnificent about him. He moved with a natural poise and powerful grace. He was not a man she could ever best unless he allowed it. And those memories! They tugged at her heart and made her wistful for those innocent times. But war and the passage of years had changed everything. "Yes, I'm set on Wycke."

"Fine." Was it her imagination, or did he appear disappointed? Now he was frowning at her again. "Why must it be only one Season? Are ye in that much of a hurry to wed?"

"No, but..." This wasn't at all what she wished for herself. "Poppy and Olivia are now married."

"And ye have no wish to be left behind?"

She opened her mouth to deny it, but pursed her lips instead. Thad wasn't off the mark. And he'd asked the question gently. She didn't have to respond like a Harpy every time he engaged her in conversation.

"They look so happy," she admitted. "It isn't merely that they now have husbands or have elevated their status. They've found love. The right sort of love that has opened up a world of possibilities for them. Have you noticed? Poppy and Olivia glow. They're like incandescent stars. They've married men who will be true partners to them, who will appreciate their hopes and dreams, and encourage them to reach as high as they wish."

"Loopy, lass. I don't think anyone can hold ye back once ye set your mind to do something."

She glanced at the book now open on her lap. "It isn't true. I am constantly thwarted, especially by you."

He laughed. "Are ye serious? Ye've bested me at every turn and have been doing so for years. Pip isn't the only diabolical Sherbourne. The lad is a saint compared to you."

She gasped. "How can you say that? Other than the tadpole incident, I've mostly been on my best behavior."

"Hah! Who was it that stole my clothes while I was swimming in this very pond?"

"That was eight years ago. I was a mere child." She struggled to suppress the bubble of laughter threatening to come out.

"Ye were an imp who led her own friends astray. Poppy and Goose, those sweet girls, would never have thought to do such mischief." He tucked a finger under her chin and gently nudged her mouth closed. "But there ye were, still a skinny, little thing no bigger than a curly-haired pixie, daring them to take on yer brother and his friends. Ye left us naked and stranded in the water."

"It was a prank, that's all. Harmless, as it turned out since Goose refused to steal Beast's clothes." She rolled her eyes. "She neatly folded them instead. Can you believe it?"

"Aye, that's because she's too good-hearted ever to consider doing anything wicked. Poppy, too. But ye got her to steal Nathaniel's clothes." He laughed again, a merry rumble that rose from deep within his chest. "I don't know how ye managed to bring out the evil in that gentle girl."

"It wasn't evil. It was daring. I knew she had it in her." She raised her gaze to his, proud that she'd brought out the strength in her friend, even if it was for a silly prank.

"Och, Loopy. Ye'll make yer mark on the world and no one's going to stop ye."

She shook her head and her smile faded. "A husband could stop me, couldn't he? That's why I need to get this right."

He put his arm around her. "All the more reason why ye should take yer time. Go on, read me the chapters. We'll make certain ye get it right."

Her gaze fell back on the book, but she felt Thad studying her. She liked the weight of his arm around her shoulders, so solid and assuring. She understood what he was thinking. *Don't leap into anything. Choose wisely, Loopy.*

She wanted to do just that, but her thoughts were in a muddle. The Book of Love claimed one's brain controlled one's feelings, but if that were so, then why did her heart respond every time she was near Thad?

Logically, he was wrong for her.

But her heart wasn't following her brain's instruction. The traitorous organ cried out for him and ached whenever he wasn't around.

The ache sprang from somewhere deep within her, some sort of eternal fountain bubbling inside of her. If circumstances were different, her choice would be easy. Thad. He would be the one she could love.

But falling in love with him meant giving up her family and friends, giving up the life she'd been raised to live, the only one she knew. All these years, she'd been trained to step into the role of countess and move about in Society.

What did she know about sheep?

Or life in the Highlands? Could she live on some barren hillside? That she adored the countryside was of no moment. The gentle Cotswolds was not the same as the cold and barren, windswept Highlands.

"We've already explored the sense of sight." She buried her face in the book, pretending to scan the chapters while trying to bring her scattered thoughts under control. His arm was still wrapped around her.

Of course, it meant nothing to him. But, oh, sweet heaven! It felt nice. "The sense of touch is next, but I've been warned it is dangerous. Shall we skip over it for now?"

"As ye wish, lass." He removed his arm from her shoulder and held his hands up in mock surrender.

"I wasn't complaining. I appreciate your attempt to console me. There, I've given you a compliment. Try not to fall off the log in a swoon." She already missed his touch, even though he hadn't meant anything by it. "Scent is next." She nudged him playfully and grinned. "Don't you dare tell me I smell like a sausage patty. Be serious now. What scents-that are not food-appeal to you?"

He shook his head and groaned in jest, but after a moment, she saw that he was giving the question serious thought. "I like the scent of pine. It fills the Highland air. It's a naturally pure fragrance. I like the scent of leather and horses, of course. They're familiar and comforting to me. I suppose I'd be a failure as a dragoon if I didn't like them."

She stifled a smile, realizing why this big Scot tugged at her heart. She'd been trying to get him to think about love, and he was going on about the Highlands and his horse. "I meant scents of a woman," she said gently, hoping to nudge him in the right direction.

He chuckled. "Och, I see. Well, if she doesn't have dog's breath or smell like mare's sweat, I would be satisfied."

"You're doing it again." She frowned at him.

He raked a hand through his hair. "Doing what?"

"Being dense, of course."

"Loopy, ye're asking me to give opinions on matters I know very little about. My time hasn't been spent in a London ballroom arranging trysts with unhappy, overly-perfumed women. Or sniffing every debutante paraded before me. I've been around men mostly. And the few women I've...met, they're not fine ladies and certainly not the sort I would ever consider courting."

"I thought you had a sweetheart."

"No." He shook his head. "Why would you think that?"

"Because you said so."

He frowned. "Och, lass. I never said any such thing. What made you leap to that conclusion?"

"Obviously, my mistake. But you're of marriageable age, and..."

Handsome as sin. "I'm sure the Earl of Caithness will be securing a wife for you upon your return."

His frown deepened. "He'll be doing no such thing. I'll choose for myself."

"Of course. I didn't mean to suggest..." She tamped down her inexplicable elation and returned her thoughts to the task at hand. She nibbled her lip, wondering how to get the right answers out of him. "Let's try this again." She tipped her head to give him access to her neck. "What scent am I wearing and what do you think about it?"

He leaned close and inhaled. "Och, that's nice. A hint of lavender."

She tried not to melt into a puddle as he began to trace his finger along the curve of her neck. Then he gently cupped the back of her head and slowly drew her toward him. His lips were so close...was he going to kiss her? She felt his warm breath caress her ear. It felt playfully seductive and ticklish. "What else, Thad?" she whispered, hardly able to speak.

Please, kiss me.

"Lavender, that's your soap. But your natural scent is..." His lips grazed her neck when he inhaled once more. "Strawberries."

"Food? Seriously?"

"Ye asked me, lass. And that's what I'm telling ye." He drew away, but only slightly. "As a little girl, yer scent was wild strawberries. That's what ye reminded me of back then, an impertinent little strawberry growing wild among the hedgerows. Tart on the outside, but when ye bit into it, ye found something unexpectedly sweet."

Had he just given her a compliment?

Penelope held her breath, for once not daring to speak. Thad was obviously in earnest, and though his words would not win accolades for poetic perfection, they captured her heart for their frank simplicity.

He took another deep breath. His eyes were now closed and his lips remained temptingly close. Thank goodness, he could not see the effect he was having on her. "I don't know, Loopy. Ye still have a little of the strawberry in ye. But now…ye also remind me of a sun-kissed lavender flower. That's what ye are. Soft colors. Delicate petals. The prettiest bloom in an English garden."

Lavender also grew in Scotland, nourished by cool, mountain waters and gentle breezes. Surely, he was aware of that. So why not call her the prettiest bloom in a Scottish garden? Or any garden?

Did they have gardens in Scotland?

She didn't know, because she'd never given it a thought until this moment.

No matter. Thad was no fool. He'd mentioned English gardens on purpose, wanting to remind her she belonged in England and not with him.

It pained her, but he was right. "So, lavender is a good scent for me."

He opened his eyes and studied her. His lips twitched upward in the hint of a smile. "Aye, lass."

She wanted to ask him what else, but this was Thad. He wasn't a rake, didn't consider women a game sport. Lavender and strawberries were all she'd get out of him.

When he looked at her with those dark, gleaming eyes, and touched her with the rough pads of his fingers, it seemed enough.

He shook his head and eased away. "What's next?"

He reached over to flip the pages to the next chapter, but she stopped him. "We're still on scent. I haven't had my turn yet."

"Ye're thinking to sniff me?"

She rolled her eyes. "Be still my heart. I'm swept away by your romantic words."

"Fine, mock me if ye wish." He gave a groaning chortle. "Why must we smell each other?"

"Ugh, Thad! We aren't rutting boars. Can you not phrase it more politely? The bond cannot be made if it only goes one way."

He tilted his head to give her access to his neck. "All right, give it a sniff. Be gentle with me. I'm delicate."

She smothered a laugh. While Thad had his elegant moments, mostly he was a plain-speaking, rough-around-the-edges Scot who would never be transformed into a gentleman. Nor did she wish him to be. She found his irreverent wit appealing.

And despite his utter lack of poetic refinement, there was something quite romantic about his gruff cooperation.

"Well, lass?"

She placed her hands on his shoulder to balance herself as she leaned forward to breathe him in. *Mercy.* "Musk. Fresh lather from your shave. A hint of saddle leather." She traced the line of his neck. "Your skin's hot."

"I'm a Highlander. This Cotswolds heat isn't for me."

Her heart skipped beats. Of course, why did it keep slipping her mind? He had no wish to stay in England. He wanted rugged mountains and icy lochs. Those were his natural scents, those of raw, rugged pine forests, their tree roots anchored to ancient mountains formed of earth and rock. He was also the cool waters of the Highland lochs that poured down from the mountains and stretched across the crags and hills toward the sea.

"A musk deer and a lavender flower," she murmured, wondering how those fit. Deer usually did not like lavender, considering the scent unpleasant. Did Thad feel the same?

He seemed to understand what she was thinking. "Loopy, I'm merely wearing the scent. I'm not actually a musk deer."

"And I'm not a delicate flower? Is that what you're saying?"

"Och, ye're a stubborn lass. Dinna I just spend the better part of an hour complimenting you?"

She laughed. "It wasn't more than a minute or two, but yes. You were quite eloquent and I appreciate your helping me out. Thad, did the experiment really feel endless and suffocating to you?"

"Endless? Yes. Suffocating? Perhaps, lass. I'm not good with expressing myself. Don't know if any man is." He glanced at the book. "And these pages are all about feelings. Men don't like to talk of them, much less think of them. Most men would prefer to be kicked in the head by their horse."

She sighed.

"And what's this opening passage about? I still don't understand it. A man's sense receptacles. It sounds lewd. What the hell is that?"

Despite posing the question, he did not give her time to respond before continuing. He began to recite the passage she'd already memorized since she'd read the book several times over. She'd read it to him earlier, but it had obviously stuck in his craw and not gone down well at all. "Love does not come from the heart but from the brain. It is the brain that sends signals throughout the body, telling you what to feel. Therefore, to stimulate a man's arousal—"

He looked up and scowled at her before reading on. "To stimulate a man's arousal response, one must arouse his sense receptacles in a pleasing way. By touch, taste, sight, smell, and hearing." He snapped the book shut. "Loopy, every man is different. What works on one will not work on another. If it did, we'd all be fighting over the same woman and have killed each other already."

He tossed the book down onto the grass and rose.

She grabbed the book and scurried to stand in front of him. "You're not leaving."

"This is bollocks."

"You promised to be my test frog." She was clutching the red, leather tome to her chest, worried that he would do something rash and toss it into the water. Were all men such idiots when it came to feelings? "We haven't performed the most important experiment yet."

He raked a hand through his hair. "What are you talking about?"

She clutched the book tighter and took a deep breath. "The kiss."

"Wycke's kiss?"

He could be such a dolt at times. She wasn't thinking of Wycke, hadn't thought of him until Thad mentioned him just now. Yes, she'd raised his name as the object of her marital desires, but it was the big, handsome Scot in front of her who'd captured her attention.

Always.

This exercise was more about forgetting Thad and less about finding another man to fill her dreams. Not that Thad filled her dreams.

Well, only lately.

In truth, all the time now.

She hoped it signified nothing. After all, she'd always thought of Thad. She considered him one of the Sherbourne family. She'd looked forward to seeing him when he came home with Nathaniel during their school recesses. And most holidays. She missed him when he did not join them. And worried about him whenever Nathaniel returned home alone. If Thad wasn't with him, it meant he'd stayed behind at school.

The thought of him walking alone up and down those long, empty halls used to make her cry.

Those times, she would go out of her way to write to him and tell him about her holidays and how she hoped his had been jolly, too. She tried to sound cheerful and engaging, although she knew his holidays must have been terribly sad and lonely.

Sometimes, she would include a drawing or silly article along with her letters. Once in a while, she would send a tin of raisin scones back to school with Nathaniel. But they were meant for Thad, and she'd had to extract a sacred promise from Nathaniel that he wouldn't eat them.

"Not thinking of Wycke," she assured him.

"Good." He slipped the book out of her hands and set it aside. Then he took her by the hand, enveloping it in his big, rough paw, and led her toward the copse of trees by the water.

She held back. "Why are you taking me there?"

"So no one can see us. I'm not going to toss ye into the water, if that's what has ye worried."

She wasn't worried, just confused. She trusted Thad. "So no one can see us do what?"

Was this it? His moment of revenge for knocking over his chair. "Thad, this is ridiculous. If you think to–"

"I'm going to kiss ye, Loopy."

Her heart shot into her throat and her eyes popped wide. "What?"

"Ye heard me. Isn't that what ye were just talking about? We were getting to it next anyway. It's the essence of this book, isn't it? The sensations of love. The touch of love. I suppose a kiss is more the *taste* of love, because my mouth will be on yours and–"

"A kiss? On the mouth?"

He arched an eyebrow. "Do ye want me to kiss ye or not?"

"Of course, I do." Perhaps she'd sounded a little too eager, the sharp intake of air giving her away. "For the experiment, of course. Even if every man is different, I'm still me and I have to figure out who is right for me."

He nodded. "I agree. That's the entire point. And while I'm kissing ye, neither of us needs to be talking."

"Gad, you're an oaf." She rolled her eyes again.

"I know, lass." He caressed her cheek. "But I don't mean to force ye. We can put it off, or never do it, if ye don't wish to."

She liked the way his thumb was making a lazy swirl against her cheek. She liked standing beside him. Mostly, she liked the idea of kissing him...perhaps too well.

Heavens, was he really going to do it? "I wish to, Thad."

He cast her a gentle smile. "Come along then. I don't want anyone watching us. Or interrupting us while I give ye a proper first kiss."

Her knees felt as though they were about to buckle.

Her bones began to melt.

A proper kiss. Yes, this handsome Scot would know how to do it proper. Could she hold herself together long enough for him to complete the task? "What makes you think it's my first?"

He shook his head and laughed. "Isn't it?"

Heat rose in her cheeks and spread across her face to the tips of her ears. "Yes, but don't you dare make fun of me about it."

His expression suddenly sobered, and he regarded her with a tenderness she'd rarely seen in him. "Nay, lass. I'm honored ye've allowed me to be yer first."

"It had to be you, Thad. It couldn't have been anyone else."

He nodded.

"Will you give me a second kiss, too?"

"I'm at yer service, lass. As many as ye wish."

LORD, HELP HIM!

Did all sense leave him every time this girl stood near him?

As many kisses as she wished? What idiot would give such an answer? He doubted he could contain himself with one, but to offer her more? Och, if he allowed his low brain function to take over, he'd have her naked with him in the water, the two of them spawning like frenzied salmon.

Of course, Nathaniel would shoot him.

He'd load the weapon to be used against him and hand it to Nathaniel himself.

He shouldn't have taken her by the hand and offered to kiss her.

Blessed saints! Her eyes were already closed and her face was tipped up in expectation of this monumental event.

He took her into his arms and ran his thumb lightly across her lips to ease the tension in them, for they were tightly pursed. "Smile, lass. This won't hurt."

"Thad..." She looked ready to cry.

He was experienced and yet still scared. She had to be terrified.

There was too much history between them for it not to mean something. For him, it was petty jealousy. She wanted Wycke.

He wasn't happy about it, but so be it.

Wycke would offer for her, was there a doubt? Who wouldn't fall in love with Loopy?

He refused to consider what else Wycke might do to her once they were married.

But Wycke was not getting her first kiss.

That would be his to treasure.

He cupped her face in his hands. *Beautiful face. Face of an angel.* He closed his eyes and kissed her gently. Well, he'd meant to be gentle, but he was swept up in a maelstrom of desire the moment his lips touched hers. He crushed his mouth to hers and wrapped his arms around her to draw her up against his body.

She responded by sliding her arms around his neck and pressing herself closer.

Lord, she's soft.

He felt the give of her breasts against the solid wall of his chest.

"Thad...my heavens." Her whispered moan undid him.

He lifted her into his arms and deepened the kiss, pouring every memory, every yearning ache, every smile, into it. Every sweet moment of laughter. The fullness of his heart and the joy she gave him. All of him, into this one kiss.

It should have meant little to him...a kiss as a favor to his friend's sister. A kiss meant to be an experiment and nothing more. *Mother in heaven.* It meant everything to him. Penelope. *This girl.* There was no one like her.

She had the spirit to kick the chair out from under him and the heart to show him more kindness and care than anyone alive.

He didn't want to give her up. She was his heart's desire.

How does an oaf like me win this girl?

He wanted to be the one to guide her, to arouse her unexplored passion. He wanted to be the one to introduce her to sensations of love she'd never experienced before. He wanted to touch her and breathe her in. Strawberries and lavender. He felt a raw, savage need to know her in every sense, to cup her lush breasts and hold them in the fullness of his hands.

To claim her body as only a husband should.

He wanted to marry her.

He wanted her forever.

He felt the fire building inside of him and knew they'd reached a danger point. He had to draw away. End the kiss.

But he couldn't let go. It had nothing to do with the hot need to explore her body. Aye, he wished to do that. Not for a mere afternoon.

He wanted a lifetime.

This girl was in his soul.

Sweat beaded across his forehead.

His shirt was damp.

He felt along Loopy's body. Her gown was damp as well. From the heat of the day or his fiery torment? Or was she experiencing a fire of her own?

Neither one of them would break off the kiss to ask. Neither one would let the other go. This was truly madness. In another moment, he'd strip her out of her gown and set her down on the soft, grassy earth to… Lord help him, he wanted to settle his big body over her and bury himself inside of her.

Low brain function out of control.

"Thad! Thad! You have a letter!" He recognized Pip's high-pitched shouts piercing the fog of his desire.

The boy continued to call his name, now louder as he drew closer.

Thad groaned as he ended the kiss and stepped away from Loopy. "Och, lass. Let me help ye. I've made a mess of ye with my big, oafish hands."

She let him.

The realization struck her as well. Her cheeks turned fiery. "I…"

"It's all right, lass. Neither of us was thinking, were we?" Her hair had come undone, the pins falling out as he'd plunged his fingers in her silken locks. The bodice of her gown was... "Let's tuck... I dinna mean to... Yer lacing, let me. I can tie it faster."

"Thad! Thad!" Pip called again, now closer.

Penelope put her hands to her hair and sighed in dismay the moment he'd righted the bodice of her gown. "He'll notice I'm still a mess. My braid is undone. Where are my pins?" She fell to her knees and began to feel along the grass. "Here are three." She hopped up and quickly drew her hair back and began to wrap it atop her head. "Help me, Thad. There isn't time to redo the braid. I'll just put it up. Stick the pins in. Quick!"

He stuck them in the best he could, then without thinking, he kissed the exposed arch of her neck. *"Mo cridhe,"* he whispered.

"It's Celtic. What does it mean?"

"Thad! Where are you?" Pip was upon them now.

Thad stepped away from Loopy as the boy burst into the copse. He moved in front of her to give her another moment to put herself together. "Over here, lad. What is it?" He strode out from among the trees and led the boy toward the fallen log under the large oak.

The Book of Love was sitting closed on the trunk where he'd left it. He picked it up and tucked it securely under his arm before Pip could get his hands on it. He doubted the lad would toss it into the water as a prank, but one could never be sure what was going through Pip's active mind.

"Nathaniel sent me down here to fetch you," he said between gulps of air as he struggled to catch his breath. "A messenger with a letter from a man with a castle came for you."

Thad's heart began to pound. "Castlereagh?"

Pip nodded.

He took off at a run, book in hand. He ought to have waited for Loopy, or at least returned the book to her, but he would leave it in

Soames's safekeeping. The butler could be trusted to keep it safe for the next few minutes.

He tore into the house and burst into Nathaniel's study. Beast was there as well.

"Nathaniel?"

"Here, it looks official. Shall we give you privacy?"

Thad nodded.

Beast slapped him on the shoulder. "We're here if you need us."

They were his best friends, and he had no secrets from them. But if the news was bad, he did not want anyone watching him fall apart, not even these men he trusted with his life. His hands shook as he opened the letter. It contained a few simple lines. *The Greys to remain in France. Return to London for your orders. Funeral services to be performed here before burial in Caithness.*

He felt ill.

Who had died? More than one officer since *services* was the plural. His brother and both his cousins were officers in the regiment. Typical of Castlereagh to ignore the most important details. He crushed the note in his hand and crossed the study to open the door.

He'd leave within the hour.

"Thad?"

Penelope had just walked into the house. The Book of Love was now in her hands. Good, Soames had returned it to her safekeeping. "Not now, Loopy. I have to pack for London."

She followed him as he continued across the hall and up the stairs. "For how long? What happened?"

He raked a hand through his hair. "I don't know. Funerals is all Castlereagh mentioned."

Her hand went to her throat. "Oh, Thad. Is there anything we can do?"

"No. I'll send word once I learn more. I may not be back in time for Goose's party. Wish her happy birthday for me, and..." A jolt of raw pain shot through his chest. "Good luck with Wycke. He's a fool if he doesn't offer for you by the end of the week."

He didn't wait for Loopy's response.

He didn't want polite thanks for his good wishes.

He had no wish to see her happy with another man. He wanted Loopy for himself. But that wasn't going to happen, not when he'd likely be ordered back to France or up to Caithness to bury his kin. Was his brother among the dead? His cousins?

He felt her gaze bore into his back, but he refused to turn around. Looking at Loopy would only break his heart, the little of it that wasn't already torn to pieces. *Mo cridhe.* He'd let those words slip out after kissing her.

She didn't know what they meant, but Pip's governess was Scottish and would know. Loopy had only to ask her.

Mo cridhe.

My love.

CHAPTER SIX

T HAD NOTICED THE tears streaming unabashedly down Loopy's face as she watched him lead Thor out of the stables. His saddlebags had already been secured and all that was left to do was bid farewell to his friends.

It saddened him that he might not see them again for years.

Perhaps never again.

The lass was not alone in watching him, for all the Sherbournes as well as Beast and Goose were here to see him off. "Stay at my townhouse," Beast offered. "Aunt Matilda is in residence and she has a full staff in place to take care of you. It'll be more comfortable than a regimental barracks."

"Thank ye, I might take ye up on the offer."

Nathaniel stepped forward. "Same here. Anything you need, just ask my man of affairs in London and he'll see it is done."

"I will," he said with a grateful nod before turning to the others. He kissed Goose, Poppy, and Lavinia, and ruffled Pip's hair. "Remember, lad. Take it slow. You and Monarch have to get to know each other before ye attempt any tricks. It isn't only a matter of keeping ye safe, it's Monarch's safety at risk as well."

Pip cast him an earnest nod. "I will. I'll take good care of him."

He ruffled Pip's head again. "Good lad." He bent down and gave him a hug.

He lifted Periwinkle in his arms and gave him a light rub on the belly. "Ye take good care of Loopy," he whispered before patting him on the head and handing him back to Lavinia.

Then there was no one left but Loopy.

Before he could figure out what to say, she threw herself into his arms. "Oh, Thad! Take care of yourself. Write to us. Let us know what's happening."

He took her into his embrace, his heart swelling with an onslaught of feelings he dared not show. "I will, lass."

"We packed some meat and fruit for you, and a few scones. We know you'll be hungry on the journey."

He chuckled. "I'm always hungry." Mostly for the angel in his arms, but food was the next best thing if he couldn't have Loopy with him on the ride to London. She was using 'we', but he knew that any comforts provided were all her doing. She'd always been thoughtful in this way, even as a little girl. Her letters. Her handmade gifts and drawings.

He eased her out of his arms. "Life will be dull without ye."

She smiled at him and nodded. "You look so handsome in your uniform. Stay safe, Thad. Send for us if you feel the need for family around you."

"I will, lass." He gave her one last hug, a quick peck on her soft cheek, and then mounted Thor. His heart pounded like a war drum in his chest. He wanted to say more to her, but the words caught in his throat.

He merely nodded to them all.

Loopy was still crying.

He couldn't bear to see her sad.

Neither could Poppy and Goose, it seemed. They moved to stand beside her. It eased his heart to know her friends would look after her.

Soon, Wycke would be the one to look after her.

He rode off before anyone noticed the watery glisten in his own eyes.

His ride was uneventful save for a quick downpour in the middle of the day. Fortunately, he'd stopped to rest Thor at one of the roadside inns outside of Oxford. Thor was already in the stable, being fed and watered when the worst of the rain arrived. As for himself, he was comfortable and dry, seated alone in the inn's taproom nursing a pint of ale while listening to the patter of raindrops and the whistle of the wind against the windows.

Pick-pock. Pick-pock. Pickety-pock.

He rose once the downpour was over. The rain had trickled to a light mist that followed him the rest of the way to London. The ground was muddied, so he'd had to ride slower than he'd liked, delaying his arrival. By the time he entered the sprawling city, it was too late to call upon Lord Castlereagh. He left their meeting for tomorrow and made his way to Beast's townhouse. Lavinia had given him a letter to bring to Beast's aunt, the dowager Duchess Matilda, and he would sooner disobey an order from Castlereagh than disappoint Lavinia.

Also, once Castlereagh got his hands on him, there might be no time to call upon Beast's aunt. He did not wish to leave the letter to just any messenger. Although it contained no important government secrets, it was his last connection to those he considered as close as family.

Matilda was at home when he arrived.

He'd intended to deliver the letter and then ride to the regimental barracks, but the grand lady would not hear of it. "You'll stay here, of course."

She ordered Beast's staff to take his saddlebags up to his guest quarters as soon as the room was made ready. After washing the dust of travel off himself and changing out of his uniform, which was taken by one of the butlers to be cleaned and pressed, he went downstairs and was shown to Matilda's elegant, private parlor by yet another butler. "I'll let Her Grace know you've come down."

He was offered refreshments which he gladly accepted, for he hadn't eaten in hours. He was thirsty, too. The long ride had left his throat parched. He settled in one of the elegant silk chairs and glanced around as he casually sipped an expensive wine out of an even more expensive crystal glass. Beast was Duke of Hartford, and although he'd never once made Thad feel inferior, there was no overlooking the wealth and power that came with the title.

The furniture and furnishings even in Matilda's private parlor were all museum pieces. The vases, the paintings, the silk chairs, and fireplace mantelpiece. The carpet and wall tapestries. All were the finest a duke's blunt could provide. Beast's entire townhouse was furnished with exquisite antiques.

Same could be said of Nathaniel. He was Earl of Welles and possessed a vast estate and homes as fine as Beast's.

Indeed, everywhere Thad looked, he was reminded of all he lacked. He did not care about it for himself, but this difference in wealth and status was a stark reminder that Loopy was better off without him. She'd be Lady Wycke soon, lady of another fine estate.

His home in Thurso was a drafty, stone manor attached to a fallen-down-rubble-of-an-ancient fortress. He was blood relative to the Earl of Caithness on his father's side, but he knew little of his mother's side. After his mother had died in childbirth, something for which he was solely to blame, Caithness and her family had feuded.

He'd been a mere babe and only learned bits and pieces of what had transpired from his brother and cousins. They'd been young as well and could only relate snippets of the gossip they'd overheard, some of it quite cruel. He'd long since stopped listening to any of it. He had no idea what was truth and what was a fishwife tale.

What he did know was that the Hume clan's territory was in the Scottish Lowlands. To a proud Highlander like the Earl of Caithness, that was reason alone to pick a fight. Thad didn't know which earl had started the feud, probably both were to blame, for that seemed to be the prideful, Scottish way, hate the other clans unless you unite to hate the English. It had been this way for centuries.

In any event, it no longer mattered to him. Whatever the reason, the fact remained, he'd never met the Earl of Hume who was his only surviving grandfather. Now that he was an adult, it was too late for him to form fond childhood memories with Hume or any of his mother's clan.

Nor would there be any formed in his adult life, for Hume had never attempted to contact him. As far as the earl or any of his clan was concerned, he simply did not exist.

"Thad, dear boy. Have you settled in comfortably?" Matilda swept in with regal dignity, the short train of her gray silk gown held in one hand as she held out her other bejeweled hand for him to bow over it.

"I have, Your Grace. Thank ye for the hospitality."

"Always a pleasure to see you. What brings you to London?"

"Business with Lord Castlereagh. But I'm too late to call upon him this evening. I appreciate your allowing me to stay here."

She shook her head, causing her fashionably styled curls to bob about her plump cheeks. "You are welcome for as long as you wish to remain."

He thanked her and gave over the letter Lavinia had written her.

She set it aside on her writing desk that was tucked in a corner of her parlor, and then walked back to his side and settled on one of the blue silk chairs beside the fireplace. She motioned for him to take the matching one beside her. The night was warm and damp. There was no fire lit, nor did one need to be lit to heat the room. But it was a cozy corner where the two of them could speak quietly without being overheard.

He expected their conversation to proceed with a polite recounting of his time spent at Sherbourne Manor and a comment about Beast and Goose in their wedded bliss, but Matilda surprised him by suddenly casting him a sober look. "Thad, dear. Are you aware that both the Earl of Caithness and Earl of Hume are now in London?"

He sat up sharply. Hadn't he just been thinking of them? "Are ye certain?"

She nodded. "They arrived earlier today. Separately, of course. They won't speak to each other."

He shot her a wry grin, finding it amazing that a dowager who rarely left her home knew as much about the comings and goings of these earls as the best trained agents of the Crown. "Do ye happen to know why they're here?"

He expected that Caithness had been summoned for the same reason Castlereagh had ordered him to London. To bring back their dead kinsmen, give them a proper funeral service with all the military honors afforded to officers, and afterward, escort their bodies back to their beloved Highlands for distinguished burial.

But the Earl of Hume was a Lowlander. He had no men that Thad was aware of serving in the Greys.

"They're both here to see you," Matilda said, further surprising him.

He arched an eyebrow. "Me? Why?"

"I have my suspicions, but I dare not say. I could be wrong."

Thad snorted. "Ye rarely are, Your Grace."

She waved the comment off with a dismissive shake of her ringed fingers. "How much do you know of your mother's family?"

He shifted uncomfortably in his chair. "Nothing." After a moment, he leaned forward and regarded her with hopeful curiosity. "I won't deny that it's left a gaping hole in my heart. My mother's blood runs through me as well, but Caithness forbade our kinsmen to speak of her or her clan. Ye seem well informed about them. Please, tell me what ye know."

"I'M NOT HEARTSICK over Thad's absence," Penelope insisted, frowning at her friends.

Poppy's sister had arrived at Sherbourne Manor in the early afternoon and was now seated on Penelope's bed along with Poppy and Olivia. She tried not to frown at Violet who had done nothing to warrant her ire.

Quite the opposite, Violet was delightful. She hoped the girl would distract Poppy and Olivia long enough to keep them from fussing over her. How she felt about Thad was her business. What she intended to do about him was also her business. "Is Thad the nice-looking Scottish gentleman we met at your wedding, Poppy? The one who was paying a lot of attention to Miss Billings?"

Penelope felt Violet's innocent remark pierce her like a knife to the heart. "He was?"

"No," Poppy quickly replied. "That was Dr. Carmichael. Miss Billings ordered some medical books for him, but I don't suppose that was really on his mind when he asked her to dance. We have a few Scots in our midst. The vicar, Adam Carstairs, is also from Scotland."

Violet grinned. "I remember him. The one with deep, blue eyes. All the ladies were flitting about him like butterflies, offering to assist him in his charitable work and making pious comments. But it was obvious their thoughts were on him and not on any pious deeds. Oh, I know which one you mean now. Thad is the big, rugged one. He was awfully quiet."

Olivia shook her head and laughed. "He was in dread fear of Penelope. Once Poppy married, it was her turn to get The Book of Love. Poor Thad knew he was done for."

"He was never in any danger from me." Penelope hoped the ache in her voice was not evident. "He isn't even here now."

Violet cast her a curious look. "Where did he go?"

"To London, but only long enough to receive new orders. We don't know where he'll be sent next." She clasped her hands together in a failed attempt to ease her distress. Nothing would make her feel better except the return of that big, rugged Scot.

"Oh." Violet cast her a sympathetic look. "He's been a good friend to all of you. I'm sure you're all worried about him."

"We are," Olivia said, obviously aware of Penelope's turmoil and sparing her the need to respond. "But Thad is smart. He'll come out of it all right." She hopped off Penelope's bed and walked over to give her a quick hug. "It's getting late. Time for me to go home. But I'll see you tomorrow. We have my birthday party to plan."

Penelope laughed.

Poppy groaned. "It was supposed to be a surprise! What gave us away?"

Olivia grinned. "The devil-child told me, of course. Pip sees and hears everything. He was so excited about my birthday and begged to be allowed to attend."

"Pip is so sweet! I would love his company." Violet was barely sixteen and had a few more years before she would be on the market for marriage. At the moment, she had more in common with Pip. But Penelope knew this would change in another year or two when her thoughts turned to her future and finding the right man to marry.

Violet would be taken quickly, Penelope knew. She was as sweet as Poppy and just as beautiful. Her eyes were an incredible violet-blue that were hidden behind unbecoming spectacles. She had the look of a bluestocking, perhaps the makings of a wallflower despite her pretty features. But any man of discerning taste would appreciate her and love her for the good person she was.

"Of course, Pip will be allowed to attend," Olivia assured. "However, the Sherbourne footmen will have to remain on high alert. That boy is bound to do something to disrupt the party. I hope it won't be a spider in the ratafia punch. Oh, I really must go. See you all tomorrow. Let's visit Miss Billings at her bookshop after breakfast. I need another book to read."

Violet clapped her hands. "I love bookshops. I often go browsing with our cousin Lily whenever I'm in London."

"We can walk into town if the weather's nice. Otherwise, we'll take Nathaniel's carriage," Poppy said, shaking her head and grinning. "I shall never get used to the crest emblazoned on its door. I still can't think of myself as a countess. I find the notion absurd. Me? Countess Poppy?"

"Mother and Father can't quite believe it either," Violet said with a smirk. "But that hasn't stopped them from boasting."

"Oh, dear. I hope they don't overdo it. I've only been a countess for a few weeks. I haven't even thrown my first party yet." She glanced at Penelope. "You must have a look at the menu Lavinia and I have planned. Let me know if we've overlooked anything. And how do I arrange for an orchestra? What else am I missing?"

Penelope took her hand. "Stop fretting. It will be a beautiful evening Olivia will not soon forget." She called to her friend who was about to leave her bedchamber. "Olivia, you must pretend to be surprised, or our guests will be disappointed."

"I'll practice my expressions in the mirror. You may remark on my extraordinary acting performance after the party." She bid her friends farewell and hurried downstairs to find Beast.

Poppy and Violet retired to their quarters as well.

Penelope was left alone with her thoughts.

Of course, they drifted to Thad.

She missed him.

Was he thinking of her at all?

CHAPTER SEVEN

T HAD WAS GIVEN a two o'clock appointment with Lord Castlereagh the following day. He made his way through the crowded streets of London, past the houses of Parliament and Westminster Abbey, allowing Thor to move at an easy lope along the Thames embankment toward the ministry offices.

Would the two earls be there?

He was comfortable enough with his granduncle, the Earl of Caithness. But what did one say to a grandfather one had never met? *Good day, Grandfather. I'm sorry I killed your only daughter.*

He knew so little about his mother. Her name was Galen Hume. Lady Galen. She had copper-red hair and emerald eyes, or so old Fiona had told him one afternoon before he'd gone off to university. He'd been sitting in the kitchen, watching the toothless harridan burn their evening meal. "She met yer father at a grand ball in Edinburgh," she'd whispered, glancing around to make certain they weren't overheard. "It was love at first sight for the both of 'em. Neither Laird Caithness nor Laird Hume were happy about it. Yer father was forbidden to court her. Yer mother was forbidden ever to speak to him. But they defied their families, both of them thickheaded and determined. No one was going to tell them what to do."

They'd eloped, Fiona had told him.

Thad shook back to the present as he reached the ministry building. A soldier met him at the entry gate. He dismounted and handed him Thor's reins. "I'll stable your horse, Captain MacLauren. Lord Castlereagh is expecting you."

Another soldier showed him to Lord Castlereagh's office. "Have a seat, Captain MacLauren. His lordship will be in shortly." He motioned to a chair in front of a massive, paper-covered desk, and then left Thad alone to await him. Well, Thad wasn't quite alone. Two soldiers stood at attention beside the door through which he'd just entered.

He was impressed.

Their uniforms gave them away as the king's personal guards. Castlereagh was important indeed to merit this protection. Since he knew these guardsmen would not be permitted to speak to him, he strolled to the window and passed the time watching the skiffs and schooners sail down the Thames.

The Thames waters were a muddy blue. The London sky was gray. The street below was crowded and a faintly foul odor from the Thames floated upward to reach his nostrils.

What was he doing here?

He wanted to take his fallen kinsmen home and see them properly buried in the unspoiled Scottish earth where their souls would rest amid the green hills and rough-hewn crags, and the golden sun would be beat down upon their sacred graves.

"Ah, Captain MacLauren, you're here. Sorry to keep you waiting." A portly, older fellow bustled in and hurried over to shake his hand. "Do have a seat, lad. We have much to discuss."

Thad settled in the wooden chair in front of Castlereagh's desk, eager to hear what the man required of him.

"As you may have heard, your grandfather requested that I bring you home immediately after the Waterloo campaign. I expect he's told you the reason, so I won't elaborate."

He began to shuffle the papers littering his desk. Thad noticed the wood was of finest mahogany, but the elegance and obvious expense appeared lost on Castlereagh who was known for his tireless efforts to secure a lasting peace rather than for his political ambition or witty social repartee.

"My grandfather?"

Castlereagh paused in shuffling his papers to regard Thad curiously. "Yes, the Earl of Hume."

Thad emitted a bark of laughter. "Forgive me, my lord. But ye must be mistaken. Not only have I never spoken to the earl, I've never even met him. So, I'd appreciate being told why he would care if I lived or died."

Castlereagh appeared surprised. "Did Caithness say nothing to you either?"

"If the information had to do with Clan Hume, he'd rot in his grave before he ever passed it on to me."

"Oh, dear. I see. So am I to understand that you've received no information at all?"

"None, my lord. Not a word in the two months I've been back."

He frowned. "Blasted, stubborn earls. This doesn't only concern them, but will they put their pride aside to do what's right? No. They'll leave me to fix things...as if I don't have enough to do. Their petty squabbles are nothing to restoring peace throughout Europe."

He rose and came around to the front of his desk. "Thaddius, my boy..."

Thad rose as well, for he knew that look of dismissal and was not ready to leave without answers. In truth, he only wanted to know one thing. "Are my brother and Caithness cousins alive? That's all I care about."

Castlereagh cast him a sympathetic grimace. "I'm dealing with thousands of men and dozens of regiments from all over the kingdom. Welsh, Scottish, Irish, and English. Not to mention, negotiating with our European allies. I'll be sending a diplomatic delegation to Austria soon, headed by me since His Majesty trusts no one else with the assignment. Names by the hundreds cross my desk every day. I honestly don't know the fate of your kinsmen."

He pursed his lips and motioned for Thad to follow him out. "Mr. Beardsley is my head clerk, an officious little weasel, but he'll give you an answer. However, I would prefer that you wait until this evening."

"Why?"

"Because I'd rather you heard the news-whatever it may be-from the Earl of Caithness. It isn't right that it should come from a stranger. I'm dining with him and Hume at a private dinner this evening. Come with me as my guest."

"I'd rather not have my family business aired at some skinny-arsed lord's dinner party. Ye'll forgive me if I decline. Besides, what makes ye think your host will allow ye to bring me along?"

"I'm the skinny-arsed host, although I'd hardly call myself thin." He rubbed his ample belly and chuckled. "It's my dinner party. At my home. The only guests are Caithness and Hume...and now you. Gad, you Scots are an impertinent lot."

Thad ignored the comment and cast him a dubious glance. "How did that come about? The two won't walk down the same street, and ye think to seat them together at yer table?"

"I will, and they'll behave because I'll have Caithness and your grandfather–"

"Don't refer to the Earl of Hume as that to me."

Castlereagh sighed. "You Scots are stubborn and prideful, too. Have you always been this way?" He shook his head and continued without awaiting an answer from Thad. In truth, he wasn't seeking a response to the question. "You'll behave or I'll have the three of you locked away in the Tower. Don't doubt my authority to do it. His Majesty's own guards will place anyone who fails to appear or show me proper respect under arrest."

Thad ran a hand through his hair in consternation. "So, I'll be trapped with ye and those two earls? I hope the food's decent. Verra well. Until this evening. But if I don't receive answers tonight, I'll start cracking heads."

Thad returned to Beast's townhouse in no fit humor to be good company. He was relieved to be told Lady Matilda was on one of her rare excursions out and would not return until late in the evening. "I'll be going out shortly as well," he informed Beast's butler.

He started for the study, knowing his friend maintained an excellent stock of brandy and intended to grab a bottle with which to drown his frustration, only to quickly change his mind. He would need his wits about him when he confronted the grandfather he'd never met.

He climbed the stairs to his bedchamber and rang for mild refreshments instead. Tea and cakes. That would hold him until supper.

He considered donning his clan tartan instead of his uniform for this unwelcome evening, but decided against it. To wear the plaid instead of his uniform would signify his allegiance to Caithness. He did care for the old hound, but did not like that he was being used by him to get back at Hume.

He wasn't pleased with either earl at the moment, and refused to show allegiance to either of them until he received the information he wanted. It ought to have been provided to him months ago.

He rode Thor to Castlereagh's home at the appointed hour. The sun was beginning to dip on the horizon, the red-gold ball casting a pink and purple hue to the sky and clouds that loomed over the London towers and spires. Those colors caught on the water, turning the Thames an odd reddish-brown.

In the Highlands, twilight came early most of the year, but it could always be counted upon to be beautiful. The cool loch waters glistened under the fading sunlight. Here, the water was too thick with mud to shine. Instead, the sun's rays seemed to be swallowed up in the dark murk.

A thin, little man scurried toward him as he dismounted. "Captain MacLauren, thank goodness you're finally here. Everyone is growing impatient for your arrival."

Thad arched an eyebrow. "I didn't realize I was late." The chimes on St. Paul's were only now ringing to signal the eight o'clock hour.

The officious man pinched his lips tightly and tossed him a superior glance. Had he been taller than Thad, he would have been looking down his refined English nose at him. But this little weasel was short and quite full of his own self-importance. He assumed this was Mr. Beardsley, Castlereagh's clerk. "Well, your kinsmen have been here this past hour."

"What has it to do with me? I assume Lord Castlereagh had news he wished to discuss with them outside of my hearing." He wasn't surprised. Everyone had kept him in the dark, so why not Castlereagh as well?

The man led him down a seemingly endless corridor. "I thought you Scots were all about clan loyalties, even above duty to the Crown." He gave a put-upon sigh. "Never mind, I suppose you ought to brace yourself for the battle that's brewing. Lord Caithness and Lord Hume have worn us all out. We've been struggling to keep each of them from ripping the other's throat ever since they arrived."

Thad snorted. "They don't like each other. They don't like me much, either. Well, Hume doesn't."

"Are you certain? They've been fighting over you like two jungle tigers after a kill." He glanced up at Thad once more and shook his head in dismissal. "Heathens."

Thad might have taken offense if he weren't so busy trying to make sense of the actions of these earls. He refused to consider the impossible…that his cousins and brother had died, leaving him heir to Caithness. Why else would these two old goats care if he was still breathing?

Caithness liked him, he knew that much.

But what of Hume?

The man was a stranger to him, so what was his motive in coming here? Although Thad was the earl's grandson, their blood tie was through his daughter. Surely, this would put him out of the Hume line of succession. A son inheriting through his mother? It was not unheard of in Scottish title grants. Had there been the glimmer of a chance he'd assume the earldom, that Lowlander bastard would have had his claws in him years ago.

The little man was still smirking at him disdainfully. Thad's heart felt ready to explode with grief, fearing the worst for his brother and cousins. But he wasn't going to show his feelings to Castlereagh's official arse-wiper.

Why hadn't either earl thought to write to him, or call upon him at Sherbourne to report the news? He deserved to hear something, be it good or dire. Instead, he'd been dangled and played like a marionette on strings, ordered after Waterloo to return on the first ship back to England. Then ordered to Plymouth to await his regiment's return. Then left without orders other than to remain within a day's ride of Plymouth. Then ordered to remain within a day's ride of London. Then back to Plymouth. London. Plymouth.

And finally, back to London.

What in bloody blazes was going on?

They finally reached Lord Castlereagh's dining hall. Officious Clerk, as Thad had taken to thinking of the little arse, opened the door and instructed him to go in. He didn't follow Thad in, merely closed the door behind him once Thad entered.

Well, this is going to be a jolly party.

Lord Castlereagh was standing beside a massive fireplace, his back to the hearth and his gaze on the door, so he was the first to notice Thad's arrival. Two other men were standing beside him with their backs to Thad.

All three had drinks in hand.

"Good evening, lad. We've been expecting you," Castlereagh said, raising his glass in greeting. The other two men frowned as they turned to stare at him.

"Good evening, Uncle Caithness." He then nodded to the stern, white-haired gentleman who could only be the Earl of Hume. Gad, he resembled the man. Eyes, nose, stubborn set to his jaw. That irked him to no end. "Are ye both going to stand there gawking at me?" Thad frowned back at them. "Or will one of ye finally deign to tell me what's been going on?" He only wished to know the fate of his kinsmen. Were they alive? That's all he cared about. *Just let them be alive.*

Castlereagh motioned for a footman to bring Thad a brandy before he responded to the question. "Do join us, Captain MacLauren."

Thad came forward to stand between the two earls. He wasn't going to show any weakness to these old men.

Caithness gave him a friendly pat on the back. "It's good to see ye, lad."

"Good to see ye as well, Uncle. How have ye been?"

"Well, my boy. Quite well. We were all pleased to learn of yer safe return."

Yet, he'd made no effort to contact Thad. "My last orders were to meet the regimental ship at Plymouth. Do ye know when it's due to arrive?"

"Aye, lad," Caithness said. "It'll arrive tomorrow, but in Weymouth. Yer cousins will be on it. They'll be taking over the duty of escorting home the bodies of our fallen kinsmen and those too injured to remain with the regiment."

"And my brother?" Thad's heart was in his throat. His cousins were alive and that relieved him greatly, but what of Augustus? They were brothers of the half blood, having different mothers. Although Augustus was eight years older, they'd still formed a brotherly bond that all their years apart could not diminish.

Serving together in the Greys had made their bond unbreakable.

"He's been placed in charge of the Greys for now," Castlereagh said. "We're keeping the regiment on the Continent until further notice."

Thad didn't care about the rest of what would be discussed this evening. His brother and cousins were alive. So many of their kinsmen had fallen in battle. That Augustus, Malcolm, and Robbie were spared was a miracle. "My brother is an able man," he said with a nod, allowing his heart to soar, but taking care not to show his feelings to these men as they continued to stare at him. "Will I be sent back to serve under him?"

"Nay, lad," the Earl of Hume said with a deepening frown. "The notion of a Hume serving under a Caithness? Preposterous." He hadn't stopped frowning since the moment Thad strode in. "Ye were the commanding officer and commended yerself well. If ye were to be sent back, ye'd be in charge of the regiment and yer brother would serve under you. But ye're more important to us here."

"How so?" If that were true, why did they leave him dangling like a fish on a hook these past two months?

"No sense being polite about it and parsing one's words. Here's the situation." Hume cleared his throat. "It has become apparent to me that neither of my sons will ever sire heirs. One was left...without ammunition, so to speak, after an illness. He's gone through two wives and has no children. The other son is a bloody idiot."

Thad arched an eyebrow. "There are plenty of titled idiots who have sired heirs. What makes your second son any different?"

Hume shifted uncomfortably. "He always was a strange lad. Claims to have seen a vision on his way home one evening. He was sixteen at the time, no doubt making his way home drunk after a night of debauchery. Whatever he thought he saw, changed him. Vision, my arse. He was too foxed to see clearly. But he joined an order of Cistercian monks against my wishes shortly afterward, and has since pledged himself to serve God."

"Cistercian order?"

Hume nodded. "He's taken his vow of poverty...and of celibacy."

Thad wanted to laugh out loud, but knew Castlereagh would lock him up if he did. "He may change his mind," he said instead. "Wealth and power have a way of enticing a man from the path of piety."

"If ye knew yer uncle–"

"Which I don't since ye cut me off from all of ye the day I was born." He knew he was being tactless. Thoughtless and irreverent. Lord, it felt good to get the anger out. It was a mild outburst compared to what he really wished to do or say to his grandfather.

"Ye have yer mother's stubbornness."

"I would not know since ye've both seen fit to tell me nothing of her." He set down his drink and folded his arms across his chest. "Lord Castlereagh, with all due respect, I think this meeting is a bad idea. If you'll excuse me, I'll–"

"Captain MacLauren, you are not excused." Castlereagh's tone was no longer indulgent.

Thad supposed he was behaving as badly as the earls, but didn't he have a right after all these years?

Hume spoke up, his voice so low at first, Thad had to strain to hear him. "My eldest son is dying. I doubt he'll be with us by this upcoming Christmastide. And as I've already mentioned, there will be no heirs from him. My other son will abdicate the title as soon as I'm dead. The Hume lairds will see that he keeps to his promise. None of them will pledge fealty to him."

"And how is any of this relevant to me? I'm yer daughter's son."

"Unlike the English, the grants to our Scottish titles on occasion will allow inheritance to pass through the female line. Mine is such. As my grandson, ye're my next closest blood kin. Ye will inherit the title. So, I've made arrangements to secure a smooth transition when the time comes."

The little hairs on the back of Thad's neck began to tingle. "What sort of arrangements?"

"The proper succession documents are all in place. The clan leaders have all been apprised of the situation." But his grandfather was fidgeting and seemed hesitant to look him in the eyes. "Since a man in yer position must set a proper example... I've taken the liberty of...I've indicated my consent to a betrothal between you and the

Duke of Ashington's daughter."

"Over my dead body," he and Caithness said at the same time.

"A Lowlander?" Caithness remarked with obvious disgust. "If he's to marry, it will be to one of us." He turned to Thad, his chest puffed out in Highland pride. "The Duke of Braemer's daughter is–"

"I'll no' be taking any bride from either of ye. When I marry, it will be to a lass of my own choosing."

"The hell, ye say." Hume was having none of it. "It's all arranged...well, almost. We'll sign the betrothal contracts upon our return to Coldstream Castle."

"Ashington's a cowardly toadie." Caithness shot him a look of utter disgust. "He was awarded the dukedom because he turned traitor to the Scottish cause. Ye'll never breed fine sons from that clan, lad. Do as I say. Marry Braemer's daughter. That's the betrothal contract we'll sign."

To emphasize his point, Caithness pounded on the dining table, causing the neatly laid out china plate settings and silverware to clatter and clink against each other.

Castlereagh scowled at his granduncle before turning his attention back to Thad. "Sorry, lad. As Hume's successor, you'll need to wed, not only for the purpose of breeding heirs. The war has been hard on the Scots in particular. Wherever there's hardship, there's bound to be talk of rebellion. The Scots and the English have a long history of it."

Thad frowned. "Are ye suggesting we aren't loyal to the Crown?"

"I have no doubt about your loyalty, son. But there are others who cannot be trusted. We have to put a quick stop to the treasonous talk that's been spreading."

"And how will my marrying help the situation?"

"Don't ask me to explain the reason why these things work, but a wedding is just the thing to cool tempers. You're young. A nice-looking lad. Heir to an earldom."

Thad grunted in displeasure. "I'm a stranger to my own blood kin."

His grandfather cracked a smile that looked forced and insincere. "But ye won't be any longer. Ye'll return to Coldstream with me. We'll have a great celebration and I'll introduce ye to the Humes."

"But ye'll marry the Braemer lass," Caithness interjected. "Ye'll no' lie with a traitorous Ashington while there's breath left in me. A Highland lass is what ye need to breed proper heirs."

"Ye'll no' lie with a Braemer while there's breath left in me," Hume countered. "I'll no' have ye marry a rebel Highlander. The only thing they know how to breed is sheep."

"I'll no' marry either of them." Thad stepped between the two men as they raised their fists, prepared to brawl in Castlereagh's dining room. "Have ye both gone mad? Are ye that filled with hatred for each other that ye've lost all reason?"

"It's for yer own good, lad," Hume said, sounding not at all contrite.

Caithness opened his mouth, prepared to bellow a retort, but Thad's glower stopped him. "So, if I understand the two of you correctly," he said, tossing each of them another warning scowl, "I'll be condemned by my Caithness kinsmen if I marry a Lowlander's daughter. And I'll be condemned by my Hume kinsmen if I marry a Highlander's daughter."

Each earl nodded.

"Fine, then I'll marry a lass of my own choosing. She won't be a Highlander or a Lowlander."

His grandfather gazed at him in confusion. "Then what's she to be?"

"A Sassenach?" Caithness bellowed, quickly grasping his intention. "Ye can't be serious? Ye'd reject the Duke of Braemer's daughter for an Englishwoman? Who is she? I forbid it."

"So do I," Hume said with a nod, perhaps the only time the two earls ever agreed on something.

But their moment of unity was short-lived. The pair turned on each other, accusing the other of neglecting Thad's proper Scottish education.

However, Castlereagh's eyes were alight. "Who's the girl, lad?"

"Lady Penelope Sherbourne, sister of the Earl of Welles. I've already offered for her hand in marriage." The lie floated out of his mouth like water down a rushing stream. He didn't care. No one was going to foist a bride on him. He knew the girl he wanted.

His heart was Loopy's forever.

"And?" Caithness asked, his mouth agape.

"And what?" He wanted to tell them it was none of their business. But his every move was now important to them. Not only had he suddenly become Hume's heir, but he also had strong ties to one of the most important Highland clans through Caithness. He hated the politics of it, and also hated that he'd just lied to everyone.

Mostly, he worried about hurting Loopy.

He hadn't proposed to her.

But Wycke certainly would, for she was beautiful and had shown Wycke none of her spit and fire, behaving like a dull, dutiful debutante at their last meeting. If the man wanted a biddable wife, he was in for a surprise. Loopy was anything but that. Yet Wycke would never know it until it was too late.

Wycke was not the sort to tease or challenge her. She'd have no reason to show him a little of her temper. Then again, perhaps she would, and he'd be fine with it. He'd likely fall in love with her anyway. How could he not?

"I've proposed, but she may refuse me. I've said nothing to her brother yet. No point until I have her answer." He rubbed a hand across his neck, silently cursing himself not only for blurting the lie in the first place, but for now repeating and embellishing it. *Blessed saints.* He had to get word to Loopy about this mess of his own creation.

Would she play along?

It wasn't fair to ask her, but he'd make it up to her somehow. She would understand his situation and forgive him, wouldn't she? He had no desire to turn his search for a wife into a spectacle. The idea of having a string of women paraded before him like show horses roiled his stomach. "Likely she will refuse me."

Damn it, the pair were scowling at him again.

"Why would she refuse ye? Because ye're an unworthy Scot?" Caithness crossed his arms over his puffed-out chest. "Who does *she* think she is?"

"These English aren't to be trusted. They believe they're better than all of us." Hume's hands were curled into fists. "Why won't she have ye?"

"She *is* better than me. I am unworthy of her." Thad did not like the direction of the conversation. The only good to come of it was learning his brother and cousins had survived. He didn't care about the Hume earldom, except it now gave him something to offer Loopy other than merely his heart.

He could ask her to marry him with his head held high.

He would not be proposing as a lowly captain in the Greys or laird of a tiny holding in Thurso. He'd come to her as an earl's heir. A Lowlander earl, but one couldn't have everything. The Hume seat was in Coldstream, just across the border between England and Scotland.

Loopy did not want to be separated from her family. Coldstream was about a week's ride by carriage from Wellesford, but better than the month's journey it would take to travel there from the Highlands.

As for her brother's consent to the marriage, Nathaniel would approve without question. In truth, he would have approved their union if Loopy loved him, no matter what Thad's situation.

However, she wanted Wycke.

"Captain MacLauren," Castlereagh said, eyeing him like a hawk. "You are now the Earl of Hume's heir. This is your opportunity to solidify your ties to one of England's wealthiest and most respected families. Lady Penelope Sherbourne is an excellent choice. Don't be a fool and muck this up."

Hume scowled.

Caithness grunted in disgust. "I suppose anything's better than a

Lowlander. Ye all sold yer souls to the English long ago anyway."

"And what of your bloodline, Caithness?" Castlereagh eyed him sharply. "Thad's cousin, Malcolm MacLauren, will eventually inherit your title. What will you have him do? Marry a Scottish nobleman's daughter who'll bring no more than a flock of sheep to their union as dowry? Or will you see reason and have him make an important connection?"

His gaze took in the three Scots standing before him. "This is a historic moment, gentlemen. Will you meet the challenge? Unite England and Scotland through marriages that will ensure a lasting peace?"

"Why should you care, Castlereagh? You're an Irishman, and we all know the Irish have no love for the English." Caithness appeared unmoved.

"Do ye think the Crown will reward ye for all yer work? They'll toss ye aside once they don't need ye anymore," Hume muttered.

Thad took a deep breath, knowing he was about to step deeper into the mire of his own creation. But he was sick of war, as were most of the men who'd fought in the many brutal campaigns over the years. Thousands had died fighting Napoleon. Tens of thousands. And these two old goats were still bickering and ready to commit their clans to more fighting.

He wasn't certain how his betrothal to an Englishwoman would help matters, but he loved Penelope. He'd thought she would be better off with Wycke. However, this conversation had changed his perspective.

Castlereagh was eager for the match.

Indeed, if the old Irishman was to be believed, the fate of Scotland and England rested upon his shoulders.

He was a failure as her test frog.

But he'd do his best to make her a good husband.

Did he have a chance to win her heart?

He hoped so, for he was going courting...Scottish style.

CHAPTER EIGHT

"'T HAD, DEAR BOY," Matilda cried, lumbering down the stairs and calling to him as he was about to leave for Weymouth. She clutched the bannister with one hand and held the note he'd left for her in the other. She was still in her bedclothes, a robe hastily tossed on-of finest silk, of course-and matching mob cap perched atop her head.

He hadn't expected her to be awake, for it was barely break of day. "I didn't mean to get ye out of bed, Your Grace."

"I know, but I was worried about your meeting last night with those hot-tempered kinsmen of yours. How did it go?"

Thad wanted to be on his way. Thor was now saddled and standing in the street in front of Beast's townhouse. His travel bags had already been brought down and strapped onto Thor. "It went fine. Apparently, I'm somebody now."

She gave a little huff as she reached his side. "You always were. Beast considers you and Nathaniel his closest friends. He thinks of you as a brother. Take a moment and tell me what happened."

She turned on her slippered heels and motioned for him to follow her into the parlor. He had no choice but to obey, for he was not about to insult this formidable dowager. Besides, she was Beast's aunt. To insult her would be taken as an insult to Beast.

He was still in a hurry to leave, so he began talking the moment her butler shut the door to lend them privacy. "Nothing official yet, but it seems I'm the Earl of Hume's likely heir. At least, he's treating me that way for the moment. Documents have been drawn up, and the Hume clan lairds have been told." He shrugged. "I've never met any of them, and they've ignored me for all my life. I'm not certain how much of this news I can trust. However, I did also learn my brother and Caithness cousins are alive. Not that any of those old bastards bothered to tell me, although they've known it for weeks."

Matilda took his hand and gave it a light squeeze. "Thad, dear. I'm so happy for you. I know how heavily their safe return had been weighing on your heart."

"Augustus has been placed in command of the Greys," he said, feeling quite proud of his brother. "They've been ordered to remain in France for now. My MacLauren cousins, Malcolm and Robbie, will arrive sometime today in Weymouth."

"Returning with the injured." She nodded. "That's why you're impatient to leave."

"Aye, Your Grace. I'll meet their ship and then ride up with them as far as Wellesford. There's a little business I must resolve first. From there, we'll continue north to Scotland."

"What sort of business?"

He shifted uncomfortably.

She arched an eyebrow. "You'll arrive in time for Goose's surprise party. Wycke will be there, courting Penelope. I assume this is the 'little business' to which you refer. What do you intend to do about her?"

"It's complicated."

Matilda studied him for what felt like eternity before her eyes suddenly widened. "I knew it! You're in love with Penelope."

"Och, Your Grace. I said no such–"

She began to ring the little bell on the table beside her. "Of course, you're in love with her. Lavinia and I have been waiting for you to do something about it. In truth, we were beginning to despair. Chrichton!

Chrichton! We're off to Wellesford! Where is that man when you need him?"

Bollocks. What was it about women and their fascination with love? And how had she known the reason for his stopping in Wellesford? Did she have the gift of sight?

Or was he that obvious?

Matilda shot to her feet with the spring of a gazelle. "I won't delay you, for I know you must get to Weymouth. But don't tarry there. Ride to Sherbourne Manor as soon as possible. I'll leave today and hold off Wycke for you. But you must act fast. He's going to propose to Penelope and then you will lose her forever."

Thad rode out of London, holding Thor back while the roadway was crowded with carts and carriages already descending upon the town despite the early hour. He gave the big gray free rein as soon as they reached the outskirts, allowing him to gallop along the open roads.

Clouds gathered overhead, covering the sun. The air did not feel particularly damp, so Thad doubted there would be much rain to slow his progress. He'd reach Weymouth tomorrow. It would not take him long to find his regiment, for they would be housed for the night near the docks, assuming they'd sailed into port before sundown.

He broke into song as he rode, no doubt irritating Thor, for his voice was wretched. But he hadn't felt this lightness of spirit in a very long time. Soon reunited with his kinsmen. Knowing the injured in his regiment would finally be home with their loved ones. And now he had Duchess Matilda assisting him in his courtship of Penelope.

Not that he'd asked for her assistance.

Nor did he particularly want her help or anyone's, for that matter.

That Beast's aunt had taken up the challenge, responding like a mother bear protecting her cub, had left a warm feeling inside of him.

Is this what mothers did for their children?

He'd never experienced a mother's love before. Matilda's fierce determination on his behalf was not something he would easily forget. It mattered not that he could take care of himself.

He'd been on his own for most of his life. He was also a man full grown and had no intention of clinging to a woman's skirts. Still, her caring shot straight to his heart and made him feel...he supposed the best description was hopeful, happy. "What shall I sing next, Thor?"

The wicked creature tried to buck him out of the saddle. "Verra well," he said with a laugh, "no more singing. Settle down, ye crazed devil."

The rest of his journey passed uneventfully. He reached Weymouth early the following morning. A mist hung over the distant harbor as he approached the outskirts of town. But the heat of the sun soon melted away the lingering haze, and it wasn't long before the sun's rays broke through and shone upon the white-capped waters with dazzling brilliance.

As it turned out, the ship carrying his regiment was only now sailing into port. He watched it cut across the expanse of shimmering blue like a sleek leviathan.

"There she is," he said in a reverential whisper and spurred Thor toward the slip where the vessel was expected to moor.

He arrived well ahead of it, and began to pace impatiently along the wooden slats of the dock, causing them to groan and squeak beneath his heavy footfalls. Waves lapped against the pilings with a soft *slush, slush*, soon drowned out by shouts and footsteps as workers began preparing for the majestic vessel's arrival.

Thad's heart was firmly lodged in his throat as he watched ropes being tossed down, the anchor dropped, and the vessel properly secured.

His cousin Malcolm must have noticed him tramping up and down the dock, for he ran down the gangplank the moment it was dropped. He whooped with joy and hauled Thad into his beefy embrace. Thad was a big man. Malcolm was even bigger, a mountain of a man. He lifted Thad as though he were no heavier than a sack of grain, practically slinging him over his massive shoulder. "Malcolm, put me down! Gad, ye're an arse!"

When his cousin finally did so, he had a big grin on his face. "Ye look good, ye skinny runt. What happened to ye? One moment, ye're leading our regiment, and the next, we hear ye're in London. What *idjit* took command of the Greys away from ye? I know ye weren't caught sleeping with a general's wife. That's more Robbie's style. Anyway, do ye ken, yer brother's in charge now? He isn't much of a field commander, but I suppose it canno' matter much now that we're at peace. Hope it holds. The French are still restless. There could be trouble."

"Augustus can handle it." He clapped Malcolm on the back as they both headed toward the vessel to greet the others. "How's Robbie? Is he with ye?"

"Aye, but he has a lame leg. Tripped over a cannon wheel aboard ship and fell hard on his knee. So he's now on the injured list." Malcolm's grin faded and he cleared his throat. "At least he's alive. We've only brought back the injured. The dead will be returned home eventually. Wellington decided it was safest to bury them in Flanders for now. Their loved ones won't be pleased, but there's no help for it. Disease is too widespread. We've lost more men to cholera and dysentery than to actual battle."

Thad nodded. "This was my greatest fear."

As they strode up the gangplank, Malcolm continued filling him in on all that had transpired. "Well, at least we'll get the injured home faster. The best medicine for them is to see the Highlands again." He patted his breast pocket. "I have the list of the dead. As soon as we're home, Caithness and I will ride from croft to village until we've paid our respects to every last family who's lost a soldier. Have ye seen our Uncle Caithness?"

Thad nodded. "Aye, in London a few days ago."

After greeting Robbie, he told his cousins all that had happened to him in these past days. "So we'll be stopping in Wellesford while ye court Lady Penelope Sherbourne?" Robbie scratched his head. "Does she have any sisters?"

"No."

Robbie was as big as Thad, and had an eye for the ladies, just as they had for him, for he was considered quite handsome by most. "Too bad," he said with a frown. "Malcolm's also in need of a wife."

His brother cuffed him. "Worry about yerself. I'm not in need of a wife."

Thad sighed. "Aye, ye are. Robbie's right." He told his cousins the rest of Castlereagh's plans for quelling the Scottish instability.

When he finished, Malcolm grinned at him. "Are ye keen on leg-shackling yerself to Lady Penelope?"

"If she'll have me," Thad said, frowning. "I hope she will, but I've handled things badly. She won't be pleased."

Malcolm shook his head in dismay. "And what of me? Has Caithness truly agreed to my marrying a Sassenach? I won't believe it until I hear it from his own lips."

"He's set on it. He was left no choice but to agree to Castlereagh's demand. In truth, these Sassenach women aren't all bad." He ran a hand through his hair in consternation, something he seemed to be doing a lot lately. He wasn't afraid of battle. He wasn't afraid of facing an enemy. He was afraid of one thing only...facing Loopy.

His stupid lie was going to hurt her.

She'd been toting around The Book of Love, believing in connections and deep commitment, and what had he done? Told everyone about his proposal except the one person he needed to tell.

She'd never forgive him for spouting the lie.

After making a quick inspection of the injured, he and Malcolm arranged for carts to carry those who couldn't ride. Since the Greys were a light cavalry regiment, most of the men had horses brought over on the same vessel and would be able to travel fast on horseback despite their injuries. Those who'd lost their mounts in battle were assigned to ride in the carts for now.

It took several more hours to arrange for food and supplies, but all the men were eager to return to their homes, so the regiment began their journey north by midday.

Thad considered what he would say to Loopy.

Perhaps the sight of injured soldiers, and the knowledge that his cousins were alive and healthy, would temper her anger. He'd introduce her to Malcolm and Robbie, of course. Perhaps Robbie's limp would soften her heart.

She didn't have to know he'd been injured tripping on a cannon wheel.

Well, he had a few days before they reached Wellesford, for the carts would slow them down. He knew what he needed to say to her. He was a Scot, after all. Not a false-tongued London dandy. The Scottish way was to be direct. *Loopy, I love ye. Forget Wycke and marry me.*

Then he'd kiss her.

He'd already kissed her once and knew she'd liked it.

How hard could courtship be?

"HOLY HANNAH," THAD muttered two days later as he dismounted from Thor and saw Penelope marching toward him. He, Malcolm, and Robbie had ridden ahead to Sherbourne Manor, hoping to arrange an encampment for his injured men in one of the meadows outside of Wellesford.

He knew Nathaniel would agree to anything he asked. Beast and Olivia would also lend assistance, offering the field behind Gosling Hall since the land was flatter and had a stream running behind it with fresh, flowing water.

The entire regiment would arrive tomorrow. Thad had purposely left them behind, allowing them to rest overnight in one of the quaint market villages a short distance south of Wellesford. Today was the day of Olivia's surprise party, and the Sherbournes already had a swarm of guests, including Wycke and his family, to entertain.

They didn't need a horde of bedraggled Scots jumping naked in the stream and ruining their party.

"Who is she, Thad?" Malcom asked with a chortle. "That is the angriest woman I've ever set eyes upon in my entire life."

Thad arched an eyebrow and winced. "That's Lady Penelope."

"Your beloved?" Robbie snorted. "Ye'd better run. I think she's going to kill ye. I see steam pouring from her ears. Och, Thad. Ye've always had a way with women."

"Shut up, Robbie." He strode toward Loopy, hoping to draw her aside to speak in private. What had he done to rile her now?

This was going to be bad. She was already fuming and didn't yet know about his London meeting with Castlereagh and his kinsmen.

He would have to rethink his courtship plan.

"Loopy, I–"

"You wretch!" She looked ready to punch him. "Are you deranged? Do you realize what you've done?"

He held his hands up in surrender. "Och, lass. Ye might explain it to me." *Bollocks.* If she was angry now, and he hadn't a clue what spur had pricked her very pretty backside this time, she'd be furious when he told her what he'd said to his uncles in London.

"You knew the Earl of Wycke was courting me." Her eyes began to tear, but the lass had spirit and would never cry in front of him, and certainly never in front of his cousins who were strangers to her.

He took her arm, attempting to draw her toward the towering oak near the pond, but she refused to budge from her spot. His cousins were gawking at them, having too much fun over his discomfort to step away and give them a moment of privacy. "Who are those men?"

"Not important." His cousins could wait to be introduced. Calming Loopy seemed more urgent. "Has Wycke said something to insult ye, lass? I'll–"

"Him?" Her hands were curled into fists. Thankfully, she still made no attempt to swing at him. "He's been a complete gentleman. It's you who…how could you?"

"I'd answer the question if I had a clue what ye were talking about. Come with me." He took her hand, giving her no chance to draw it away, and strode to the pond and the fallen log. He nudged her onto the gnarled trunk and stuck his booted foot beside her to keep her from running off. Not that she had a mind to run. No, she wasn't finished railing at him.

"Did you or did you not tell your kinsmen that we were betrothed? And now they're both here, demanding explanations why I am entertaining Wycke's suit when I'm promised to you."

Thad's stomach sank. "My kinsmen? Ye can't mean the earls, Caithness and Hume?"

She nodded. "The very ones."

Well, that explained her temper. "Blessed saints! What are they doing here?"

"Besides checking my teeth and my gait? As if I were a filly at auction?"

He ran a hand through his hair and looked over her toward the manor house where the two old men had to be doing their worst. "Loopy, I'm sorry. I never realized–"

She jumped up and gave a shove to push him away. "Don't call me that. My name is Penelope. *Lady Penelope*. And I'll never forgive you for humiliating me the way you have."

She turned and ran back to the house.

Blasted kin had ignored him his entire life. Why did they have to take an interest in him now? He wouldn't blame Loopy if she never spoke to him again.

He returned to his cousins who were waiting for him by the front door. "Ye should have kissed her," Robbie said.

"Shut up, Robbie."

"I would have kissed her," Malcolm agreed.

Thad strode inside. He needed to find Nathaniel and explain this mess before Caithness and Hume realized he'd arrived and trapped him.

He made his way through the hall into the music room, his cousins following close behind, no doubt gawking at the elegance of this 'simple' country home. Few Scottish estates could boast such finery.

He paused to peer out the long windows that opened onto the garden.

The day was warm and sunny. Olivia's party appeared to be a lively affair. Tables laden with food were set out in the rear field between the Sherbourne garden and the back road to Wellesford. Servants were running in and out of the kitchen carrying tankards of ale, bowls of ratafia punch, and trenchers laden with meat and fish.

Much of the town was in attendance.

The sun was shining over the garden, but Thad stood in the shadows, preferring to remain unseen. He continued to peer through the music room window, easily spotting Matilda and Lavinia holding court while seated beneath one of the large shade trees.

How much had Matilda told everyone?

Periwinkle was snuggled on Lavinia's lap, as always.

Pip was in the distance, showing Monarch off to a group of village boys. Good. The lad needed to play with children his own age.

His attention returned to the two dowagers and the guests seated beside them. He recognized Lord and Lady Plimpton, Goose and Poppy. Wycke and his mother and sister. Standing just behind them were Beast and the two earls, Caithness and Hume.

Was it Castlereagh's brilliant idea to have them come here?

Nathaniel approached him and clapped him on the shoulder. "I thought I made a fool of myself while courting Poppy. You, my friend, make me look brilliant. Care to fill me in on what happened?"

"Och, Nathaniel. Ye'd better lock yer pistols in their cabinet. Loopy's angry enough to shoot me." He introduced Nathaniel to his cousins, then they all retired to Nathaniel's study to hear Thad's explanation of the quagmire he'd created for himself.

To his relief, Nathaniel seemed more amused than angry. "Wycke now believes he has competition for Penelope's affections. I suppose it's a good thing. Makes her more desirable to him. Frankly, I haven't seen much fire in the man. I'm not sure he loves her."

Thad dismissed the notion. Not all men were flaming arses such as himself. Wycke was the deliberate, cautious sort.

"Despite the fact that she presently wishes to cut your life short, Penelope is tender-hearted when it comes to you. She always has been. As angry as she is, she'll never betray you."

Thad grunted.

Indeed, he was *her* big, dumb Scot. No one was going to kick his arse but her.

"She hasn't contradicted your kinsmen, so everyone believes you've proposed to her. But she's hurt, Thad. She feels you've made a laughing stock of her."

"Och, it was never my intention. If I could take back my words, I surely would. Ye know I'd never purposely hurt the lass." He rose and began to pace. "I've loved her all my life. Ye know I have. She didn't need to test out those recipes in The Book of Love to sway me. I would have proposed to her the moment I returned to England had I anything to offer her. Until a few days ago, I had nothing."

Nathaniel poured Thad's cousins a brandy, pausing only a moment to hand them their drinks before he responded. "I would have given you my consent."

"I know, but it wouldn't have been fair to her. She's a grand lass.

She was raised to be the wife of a nobleman. She belongs in a fine house and deserves to go about in elegant Society. I would have killed her spirit by dragging her to Thurso and the hardships of a Highland winter."

"But all that's changed now," Nathaniel said.

Thad nodded. "I'm heir to the Earl of Hume, if he's to be believed. He was shoving a duke's daughter at me. Caithness was doing the same. If I'm to marry, it will only be to yer sister. I'll have no other lass as my wife."

"Well, you'll have a way to go before she believes you love her. Caithness and Hume saw to that with their inelegant meddling."

"No, it isn't the fault of those old bastards. It's my fault. I've used her poorly. Serves me right for tossing her up as an excuse. I've probably pushed her straight into Wycke's arms."

"Maybe, but there's nothing to be done about it today." He rose and started for the door. "Come on, I may as well introduce your cousins to our guests. There's plenty of food. Help yourselves. Our guestrooms are full, but Beast and Goose will take you in at Gosling Hall. How long do you plan on staying?"

"No more than a day or two," Thad said, wishing he had another week.

But that wasn't going to happen. The injured men deserved to be brought home as soon as possible. He was no longer their regimental commander, but they had been through the worst of the war with him in charge. He could not abandon them now. No matter that his cousins were capable. These were his soldiers, his brethren. He would always feel responsible for them. "We'll head north the day after tomorrow."

He doubted Penelope would forgive him by then, but all he had to do was gain her promise not to accept Wycke's proposal.

Once she calmed down, hopefully by the time he returned to Wellesford, he'd propose to her in earnest. He'd let her know his intentions before he rode off. She did not need to answer him now. He wanted to give her time to consider what marriage to him would entail.

He'd place his heart in her hands.

She could do with it as she wished, and would hopefully not crush it.

He'd love her no matter her decision.

"Thad, good to see you!" He was accosted by friends and acquaintances the moment he stepped into the garden with his cousins. After making introductions, he attempted to leave this inner circle of hell. Not that he minded Poppy or Olivia, or the dowagers, but Caithness and Hume were now standing beside him, and so was Wycke.

As for Wycke's mother and sister, they were eyeing his cousins with avid curiosity.

Malcolm nudged him. "Is Wycke's sister spoken for?"

"Not that I'm aware. Anne had no beaus as of a few weeks ago."

"She's a pretty lass."

Thad's gaze drifted to Anne Halford. She was attractive in a quiet, unadorned way. Her hair was a honey-brown and her eyes were a mix of brown and green. She was on the small side, but full-figured. In other words, Malcolm's low brain function had taken control and he was admiring the girl's breasts. He knew exactly what his big, dumb cousin was thinking. *Fertile female. Want to mate with her.*

Gad, no wonder Loopy considered all of them idiots.

He paid no more attention to his cousin's musings as Hume and Caithness approached him. "Glad ye're here, lad. It's time ye sealed this betrothal," Hume said.

Caithness nodded in agreement. "That damn Sassenach lord has been doing his best to steal the lass from ye. Good thing we were here to put him off."

More like push her straight into Wycke's arms.

"What are ye old goats doing here? I dinna invite ye to meddle in my courtship." Of course, he wasn't courting Loopy, and by the fire in her eyes when he'd seen her earlier, there would be no such thing happening until she got over her hurt and anger.

The earls ignored his comment. "Where is the lass?" Caithness asked. "I thought she left us to greet ye?"

Robbie, who was listening in on the conversation, gave a snorting laugh. "Och, she greeted him all right. The lass is on fire for him."

"Shut up, Robbie." Thad folded his arms across his chest as he returned his attention to the two old men. "I want ye gone from here. Now."

Caithness mimicked his stance. "Save yer breath, lad. We aren't leaving until she gives ye an answer."

Thad groaned.

"But rest easy," Hume said. "Ye're a handsome lad. If she seems reluctant, just kiss her as though ye mean it."

"I would mean it."

"Then where's the problem?" Caithness grumbled. "Ye can't blame us for being cautious. The fate of Scotland–"

"You came to inspect her like ye would a herd of cattle. Ye had no right."

Hume raised his hands in a gesture of surrender. "If she's to be the next Countess Hume, the lass will need to meet with my approval. Ye needn't make a fuss. She's bonny enough. Ye'll have my consent to marry her."

"And mine," Caithness assured.

"But you won't have mine," Wycke said, approaching him. "I intend to fight for her."

CHAPTER NINE

P ENELOPE WAS ALREADY regretting her decision to rejoin Lavinia, Matilda, and the others under the massive shade tree in the garden. She'd returned in time to hear the two Scottish earls approve of her betrothal to Thad, even though the big oaf had yet to propose to her.

And now the Earl of Wycke had just declared his intention to fight for her hand in marriage. She had to give him credit for his determination, or was it simple lunacy? Thomas Halford had made the declaration in front of five burly Scots, one of whom was the size of a full-grown oak tree. Malcolm was the name of that giant. Penelope hoped he was not ill-tempered, for no one, not even Thad, who was quite big and brawny himself, would be able to stop him if he decided to uproot Wycke and toss him like a caber across the garden.

"My lord, I'm–" Before she could finish her comment, a keening shout pierced the air, quickly followed by more shouts from the boys who had been watching Pip ride Monarch near the back gate.

Penelope took off at a run toward them when their shouts turned to cries of alarm. Her heart was beating wildly and the breath suddenly rushed out of her as Monarch reared on his hind legs and then bucked on his forelegs, and once again reared on his hind legs.

He was trying to toss Pip off the saddle. "Pip! Get your foot out of the stirrup!"

The boy was desperately trying to hang on, but couldn't. At this point, Penelope could only pray he would tumble off cleanly. Any broken bones suffered from the fall would heal in a short time.

But if the horse took off at a run with Pip's foot caught–

Her cousin would be dragged along the ground, likely killed the moment his head hit a rock. "Pip!"

She heard footsteps behind her and knew others were responding to the cries of the local boys. Thank goodness, Dr. Carmichael was at the party. She'd last noticed him chatting with Miss Billings. Where was he now? They'd have need of him.

Monarch was still bucking and kicking, obviously frightened by something.

What trick had the boys been attempting that got him so riled?

She reached out to grab the reins, but Monarch chose that moment to rise once again on his hind legs. The beast suddenly loomed over her with his powerful hooves flailing. She tried to scramble out of the way, but stumbled.

Then all she saw was a wildness in the horse's eyes. All she heard were his frantic neighs and heavy snorts. The breath rushed out of her as those big hooves hovered directly over her, scratching at the air before descending on her.

She tried to scream, but what came out was an ironic laugh. She'd never had two beaus before. No one had ever vied for her hand until a few days ago.

And now she was going to die.

"Och, Loopy!" Thad's massive arms were suddenly around her like a warm, protective blanket, lifting her out of the way as he shielded her with his body.

"Thad!" She heard a soft thud, and then felt a rippling shudder course through him, for he was still holding her body tightly against his. She knew he'd just absorbed the brunt of the horrific impact as Monarch's hooves landed on him.

He loosened his grip on her and shoved her to safety while he collapsed, with a curse, to his knees. "Bollocks, ye're the most vexing lass that ever existed."

Penelope watched in a daze as her brother and Beast subdued the frightened horse. Out of the corner of her eye, she saw Dr. Carmichael and Thad's two cousins run forward to kneel over Pip's little, crumpled body.

But in the next moment, the boy sat up with a howl.

"A broken arm," one of Thad's cousins remarked.

But what of Thad? The two earls, Caithness and Hume, were bending over him as he now lay on the ground.

She shook out of her momentary stupor. "Thad!"

She sank to her knees beside him.

Dear heaven! What had she done?

"I'll be all right, lass." She didn't believe him, for his voice was strained and pain etched his handsome features.

Wycke now stood beside him. "It's his arm, it's rotated out of the shoulder socket."

Penelope gasped, noting the odd dangle of his arm as it protruded from his now torn shirt. She wanted to call Dr. Carmichael over, but how could she call him away from Pip who had also suffered a broken bone and perhaps worse?

She didn't know what to do.

Wycke took her hand and gave it an assuring squeeze. "Let him take care of the boy." She followed his gaze, which was momentarily fixed on the doctor as he worked on a still howling Pip, and then he turned back to her. "I know how to fix his shoulder." Wasting not another moment, he knelt behind Thad and gingerly placed one hand above and one below the bone. "This will hurt, MacLauren. But only for a moment while I manipulate your arm back in place."

To Penelope's surprise, Thad readily accepted Wycke's ministration. "Och, do it. I've seen injuries such as these on the battlefield."

"What can I do?" Penelope was certain she was going to be ill, but if these men could manage to remain calm, so would she.

"Nothing," Thad said, casting her a wincing glance. "Men fall off their horses all the time. This sort of thing happens often enough in the heat of battle. There isn't a cavalry soldier alive who hasn't taken a tumble."

But Penelope knew it hadn't happened to Thad before, not while he rode with the Greys. Perhaps as a lad, when he was learning those dangerous tricks.

"Och, Mother of–"

Her heart shot into her throat as she heard the crack and pop of bone relocating in its socket. Thad's face was ashen. He tried to rise, but his kinsmen would not hear of it. "Stay put, lad," Caithness said. "Yer cousins will help ye into the house in a moment. Ye need to be in bed."

"I dinna need to be coddled. Besides, this house must be full. Not a bed to be had."

"Why must you always be so thick-headed?" Penelope wanted to throw her arms around him, but there were too many people watching. "Put him in mine." The instruction tumbled from her lips before she realized what she was saying. "I mean... Yes, my bed. But I'll move in with Aunt Lavinia. Or I'll stay at Gosling Hall."

Wycke frowned at her. "Lady Penelope, I don't think–"

"Or you can give up your guest quarters, my lord." She frowned back at him, which was perhaps harsh, for he'd just helped Thad when he could have stepped back and allowed him to suffer. They were rivals, after all. "You see," she said, softening her tone, "that's where Captain MacLauren always stays whenever he comes to visit."

"So it's more his room than mine," Wycke said with a nod. "Of course, I'll give it over to him."

She smiled at him. "That's very kind of you. Quite generous, indeed. Soames will see that all your belongings are moved to Gosling Hall."

"No." Thad gave a snorting laugh and then a yelp of pain. "Ye canno' kick the man out of his guest quarters. He fixed my shoulder."

Penelope rolled her eyes, knowing Thad was about to pull his 'Scottish code of honor' speech, which she had no patience for right now. How could she listen to his drivel when he was obviously writhing in pain? "You're hurt."

"No, lass. Just a scratch. I'll be fine in a moment."

"Your face is a bilious green." She brushed a lock of hair off his forehead that was beaded with sweat. "You almost got yourself killed, you big ox."

"Better me than you. Gad, ye're a vexing Harpy." He turned to Wycke. "Take her back to her aunt. Make sure she isn't hurt."

"I'm fine," Penelope insisted.

"Ye're trembling, lass. Sit down under the shade tree. Take a sip of lemonade, and…keep out of trouble."

She made no protest, understanding Thad's pride and knowing he had no wish to have her watch him attempt to stand up on his own shaky legs, assuming he had the strength to manage it. She turned to Wycke. "Take me to Pip first. I need to see he's all right."

"The lad's fine," Robbie said, arriving at that moment to give them a report. "Seems a harmless garden snake slithered in front of Monarch and gave him a scare."

Nathaniel now had the boy in his arms and was marching toward them on his way into the house. "Pip has fractured his arm. Dr. Carmichael set it back in place. He'll be all right. But he needs to rest in bed. How's Thad?"

"The horse kicked his arm out of socket, but its set back in now," Wycke responded. "He may need to keep his arm in a sling to allow it to heal."

Pip was softly crying, but also resisting Nathaniel's attempt to carry him inside. "I want to stay with my friends."

"Och, lad." Thad was now on his feet, albeit leaning against his two cousins, Malcolm and Robbie. "My bone popped out, too. We'll have matching wounds."

The boy immediately stopped sniffling and struggling, and his eyes lit up. "We will?"

"Aye. But go on up to yer room now without a fuss. Look at ye, with yer clothes ripped and dirt-stained. Is that any way for yer friends to see you? Addie will tend to ye."

Penelope removed the lace handkerchief she always kept tucked in her sleeve and used it to wipe away the boy's tears. "Once you're settled, we'll let your friends come up and visit you for a little while." She exchanged a look with Thad, for she knew how lonely he'd been as a child, and how his heart was now aching for Pip.

Pip was so eager for the company of friends his own age, he would ignore his considerable pain for a precious afternoon with them.

Thad cast her a tender smile before returning his attention to the boy who was now openly worshiping Thad as his hero. "Let's meet at breakfast in the morning and compare our matching wounds."

She'd never seen a brighter smile on any child.

Penelope dearly wished to kiss Thad, no matter that he'd lied to everyone about proposing to her. She was still hurt and angry for his presumption, but it paled in importance to seeing her young cousin happy.

Thad's soft gaze was still upon her.

She cleared her throat and turned away.

His kinsmen were watching them. So were Lavinia and Matilda, as well as Olivia and Poppy. Even Wycke's gaze was darting back and forth between her and Thad.

Thad didn't seem to notice or care. "Eight years of battle," he said with a light chuckle, "and nary a scratch on me. Five minutes with ye, Loopy, and I'm nearly killed."

Penelope meant to tip her chin up in defiance, but she could no longer muster any indignation. He was right. She was dangerous to him. A bloodied lip at their last meeting and now an out-of-joint shoulder bone. And Pip might have been killed. Of course, that wasn't her fault, but she blamed herself anyway. She turned away, fearing to burst into tears.

"Och, lass! I dinna mean–"

"Yes, you did." She darted into the house as the need to get away from all of them overwhelmed her, especially to get away from Thad who seemed able to manipulate her heart at will.

SINCE THAD HAD not intended to sleep at Sherbourne Manor—not that there was a jot of space available this weekend anyway—he and Dr. Carmichael were now seated outdoors in an alcove near the kitchen while the good doctor tended to his injury.

"Lord Wycke did a commendable job," the doctor muttered. "I'll bind your shoulder to keep the bone in place, but first I'll have to cleanse your wound. I see blood around your shoulder and across your back. I'm afraid Monarch's hooves tore your skin. In the shape of a horseshoe, I'll wager. You'll have to take your shirt off so I can treat it."

"I'll help ye." Robbie was by the kitchen door, flirting with several maids, but scrambled to Thad's side.

Dr. Carmichael laughed. "Fine, but not here." He glanced at the maids who'd also heard his comment and were beginning to gather around Thad. "In Lord Welles's study. That should lend us some privacy."

Robbie grinned. "The lasses will be sorely disappointed. I'll see what I can do to assuage them."

"Och, Robbie. The earl is my best friend. I'm trying to woo his sister." Thad grunted to acknowledge the poor job he'd done of it so far. "I don't need ye merrily ploughing yer way through his maidservants. Just behave yerself for once." He ran a hand through his already unkempt hair. "And where's yer brother?"

"Over there." Robbie pointed toward the rose garden.

Thad rose to his unsteady feet for a better view. "Bollocks." Malcolm was strolling with Wycke's sister. The big ox had a stupid grin on his face, while Wycke's sister gazed up at him with adoring eyes. "Has the world gone mad?"

Perhaps Monarch had kicked him in the head and he was now unconscious, merely having unsettling dreams.

But the delectable scents of roasting meat and fresh baked bread emanating from the kitchen, and the pain tearing through his shoulder in hot, intense jolts, suggested he was awake and this was not merely a bad dream that would soon end.

Was Wycke aware Anne was about to be seduced by a MacLauren?

He'd deal with Malcolm later.

Penelope was the more urgent problem. He needed to speak to her. He couldn't leave things as they were between them, for he'd unwittingly insulted her, and she'd fled to her bedchamber in tears. "I'll meet ye in Nathaniel's study in a few minutes," he told Dr. Carmichael and Robbie. "There's something I must do first."

Ignoring their protests, he marched inside, although some might consider it more stumbling in. He barely made it up the servants' stairs. By the time he reached the first story landing, he was breathing heavily.

It had taken quite some effort to maintain his balance and not tumble down the stairs.

Perhaps this was not his brightest idea.

He glanced down at himself to conduct a quick assessment of the damage. He already knew his shirt was torn at the spot Monarch's hooves had struck him. But it was also stained along the front, that deep-ground streak of grass occurring when he fell hard after the blasted beast had done his worst to him.

His body was now dripping in sweat, for it had been no easy feat to climb those stairs.

Since he felt no damp ooze down his back, he doubted he was still bleeding. But his shirt was now stuck to his skin, which meant he'd bleed again once the doctor peeled the fabric away.

He took a deep breath and groaned. Perhaps his nose was off, but between the sweat and blood and grime, his scent was hardly that of a Scottish rose.

This had to be his stupidest idea ever, but his heart ached with love for Loopy, and he needed to make her understand how he felt before he was put in bed and dosed with enough laudanum to knock him out for the night.

He started down the hall toward her bedchamber. "Loopy," he said, quietly knocking at her door.

"Go away." Her response was muffled because they were on opposite sides of the heavy wood door, but there was also an irritatingly persistent ringing in his ears and the floor beneath him had now begun to spin.

"No, lass. I cannot. Let me in." He knocked again, a little more forcefully this time. "It's me. Thad." Of course, she knew exactly who it was. No one else called her Loopy in a deep Scottish brogue. Perhaps he ought to try using her given name. "Penelope. Lass."

She still refused to respond.

Or had she? He simply couldn't hear, for the bells were no longer quietly ringing between his ears but clanging with the resounding force of Yorkminster church bells.

He waited another moment and placed his hand on the door latch. "Are ye decent? I'm coming in."

"No, Thad! Don't you dare!"

Her door was unlocked.

He marched in.

And ducked as she hurled a faded, red-leather tome at his head. He recognized it as The Book of Love. It landed with a thud in the hallway. He bent to pick it up, feeling as though every bone in his body was being stretched on a rack. After wobbling to his feet, he wiped off the little dust that had collected on the binding.

He was surprised she'd chosen this book to fling at him. Until this moment, she'd been toting it under her arm and protecting it as though it were a sacred text. Obviously, her desire to kill him outweighed her desire to find love. "What did ye do that for?"

He stepped into her room and shut the door behind him. "If ye scream, everyone will hear ye and come running. Then ye'll have to marry me."

"Don't you dare speak to me of marriage."

He smothered a grin, loving the tip of her head and tight line of her spine as she tossed him that familiar look of majestic indignation. She'd also tossed back her shoulders, which only accentuated the lush fullness of her breasts.

"How could you tell everyone that you'd proposed to me? And I was considering your offer? Did it ever cross your mind to write to me and warn me what you'd done? Perhaps apologize for it, too? And now they think you want to marry me. Coward! You're using me to avoid having to accept someone else. Did you ever consider my feelings while plotting your diabolical charade?"

Her cheeks were flushed and her chest was heaving.

She gave a grunt of exasperation. "Stop staring at my breasts, you oaf."

"Can't help it. Ye're breathing. Heavily."

"I'm angry."

"I know, lass. Ye're also beautiful, and my defenses are down. I can barely stand on my own two feet." His head began to spin faster than it had been spinning before. "Bollocks." He grabbed the bed post as the floor suddenly seemed to disappear from under him.

"Thad!" She put her arms around him. "You've turned green again."

He was about to cast up this morning's breakfast, and yet he couldn't help but think how soft and wonderful she felt against him. That he was now in a position to offer her something, she'd be his countess once he inherited the Hume earldom, was nothing short of a miracle. He wasn't going to waste this precious gift. "Och, lass. Ye smell as delicious as a raisin scone."

He kissed her on the neck. "Ye taste like…"

He'd meant to tell her that she tasted like heaven, but he never got the words out. He began to topple like a great stone tower under trebuchet siege.

He collapsed, taking her down with him.

"Thad! You big oaf!"

When he opened his eyes sometime later, he realized he was still in Loopy's bedchamber, but she was no longer beside him. Or shouting in his ear as she tried to shove his dead weight off her.

Nathaniel, Beast, and Dr. Carmichael were now hovering over him.

He moaned. "Where am I?"

But he knew.

And he also knew that he was naked under the covers. Blessed saints! What had he done to Loopy?

"Olivia and Poppy came down to fetch us after you fainted." Nathaniel was frowning, obviously not pleased by his behavior. "You really are a big, dumb Scot. Did you not realize the four of them were in here when you burst in?"

"Four?"

"Penelope, Olivia, Poppy, and Poppy's young and very impressionable sister, Violet," Beast said with a groaning chuckle. "They heard your every word. From what I gather, you made a monumental arse of yourself."

Thad sighed. "So what else is new? Seems I canno' do anything right around Loopy."

"Spectacular fail," Nathaniel agreed.

"Where is Penelope now?" He tried to get up, but his friends held him down. Although they were careful not to touch his injured shoulder, he let out a yelp as a stinging burn ran up his side and burst within his shoulder.

Now his left arm felt numb and his heart was beating so hard, he had to gasp for breath.

"Lie still," Dr. Carmichael ordered. "I'm going to give you some laudanum to help you sleep through the night."

"Penelope."

"You're not courting her today," Nathaniel insisted. "You smell like two-day old socks and you can't string two sentences together. Nor can you stand on your own two feet without heaving up the contents of your stomach."

"Where is she?"

Nathaniel sighed. "The truth?"

"Always," Thad said with a nod.

"She's strolling by the pond with Wycke."

"Damn it. And ye let her?"

"Of course, I let her. She cast me that look. You know *that look*. I wasn't about to make matters worse by trying to stop her." Nathaniel nudged him back onto his pillows when he attempted to roll to his feet. "Stay put. You need to heal before you do anything else stupid."

"But Wycke—"

"Still needs my consent to marry Penelope, which I will not give immediately. So use your bed rest productively." Nathaniel handed Thad the red, leather-bound book his sister had thrown at him earlier. "If you can keep your eyes open, read The Book of Love. I know we've told you much about it, but it isn't the same as reading it for yourself."

Beast nodded. "Most important, you have to understand exactly what it is you feel for Loopy. Are you sure it's love? Or were you just grasping for the familiar when your kinsmen and Castlereagh began making marriage plans for you?"

"Be sure, Thad." Nathaniel frowned at him. "Because I'll have to kill you if you break my sister's heart."

His friends had raised valid points.

He would read the book with an open mind. But he knew his feelings for Loopy were sincere. Was it possible his heart had misled him? He didn't think so.

But what if Loopy's heart was misleading her?

He glanced at the book, clutching it tighter in his hand.

If Olivia, Poppy, and Penelope were using it to make a man fall in love with them, then why couldn't he use it make a woman, namely, hard-headed, sinfully delectable Loopy, fall in love with him? "Aye, I'll read it."

It was a simple plan.

What could go wrong?

CHAPTER TEN

"I S LAIRD CAITHNESS always so...thick-headed?" Wycke asked Penelope as they strolled down the lane toward the pond on this sunny afternoon.

The weather could not have turned out more beautiful for Olivia's birthday party. A bright blue sky. A few tufted, white clouds. Even the wind cooperated, carrying a gentle breeze with a hint of autumn to keep them cool under the blaze of the shining sun.

The day would have been perfect if not for Pip breaking his arm during his mishap while riding Monarch, and Thad...just being Thad. Big and wonderful and protective, even though he was the most maddening man ever to exist.

She ignored the question, for speaking of Thad made her heart ache.

Other guests were walking with them, some a little ahead and others behind, so Penelope did not wish to say too much on the chance they'd be overheard.

Thad's cousin Malcolm strode beside Wycke's sister, a few steps ahead of them. The pair were engaged in their own apparently fascinating conversation, for their gazes were on each other and not on the path in front of them.

Goose, Poppy, and her sister, Violet, had run ahead and were already seated on the fallen log by the pond. But their gazes kept darting to the manor house, the upper floor, to be precise. Penelope knew they were thinking of poor Pip, who had been left in the capable care of his governess, Addie. His friends had been allowed up to his bedchamber to visit, so she knew Pip was happy, even if he was in a good deal of pain.

Penelope would have liked to remain by Thad's side, but her brother would not hear of it. Since there had already been enough excitement for one day, she decided not to argue the matter. She'd look in on Thad later.

Wycke repeated his question. "Is he always thick-headed?"

She could have agreed. Was there any doubt Thad was the most irritating, provoking man she'd ever met? Infuriating, too. She wanted to kick him as often as she wanted to kiss him. Although lately, she'd wanted to kiss him an awful lot.

Well, she couldn't admit that to Wycke. "Laird Caithness? Oh, he's..."

Ugh! Even when not here, Thad managed to rile her.

But she stopped herself from speaking ill of him. Yes, he'd made a spectacular ass of himself in front of her and her friends, finishing his impassioned bit of theatrics with an ungainly dive to the floor. That dive would have caused him even more damage had she not been there with her arms wrapped around his granite-hard body to cushion his fall. "He's a decent fellow."

Wycke shrugged. "I suppose you won't speak ill of him after he saved your life."

"It would be very rude and unforgivable." She began to nibble her lip, hoping she hadn't been too harsh with Thad. After all, he was hurt and yet, he'd followed her up to her bedchamber to apologize for teasing her. "He's a mix of exasperating and wonderful. He constantly goads me, and yet he won't hesitate to risk his life to protect me. I suppose I goad him, too. I hope he knows that I would protect him if ever his life was in danger."

Wycke clasped his hands behind his back and regarded her

thoughtfully. "I'm sure he does know it."

She nodded. "I hope so. He and I have been friends for a very long time."

"And now he's heir to an earldom and chosen you as the girl he wishes to marry."

Penelope glanced back and frowned at the two Scottish earls, Hume and Caithness, who were following behind them at a languid pace. But they were definitely keeping their hawk eyes on her and Wycke, no doubt irritated that she would deign to stroll with a Sassenach earl instead of remain weeping by Thad's bedside.

"I'm familiar to him." She sighed. "I suppose you could say I'm the devil he knows. Thad doesn't like surprises. He isn't keen on change, either. If he's forced to marry, it may as well be to me. At least, to his way of thinking."

"And what about you? How do you feel about his proposal?"

"I'd rather not speak of it. Shouldn't we be talking about you? Why do you wish to marry me? You don't know me at all."

Nor did she know him. Indeed, he could be a cruel monster, for all she knew. Yet, he struck her as a good man with a deep caring for his mother and sister. In this way, he was much like Nathaniel, keeping his family close even though he could have shipped them off to one of his many holdings and led a comfortable and carefree bachelor life in town.

The Book of Love-which she probably shouldn't have hurled at Thad-spoke of the importance of connections between two people. She and Wycke had almost no connection, yet that didn't seem to trouble him or make him cautious in his pursuit of her hand in marriage. He was an Englishman. He was an earl, one of substantial worth financially as well as morally, or else Nathaniel would not have allowed him near her. He had a pleasant mother and very sweet sister...notwithstanding, Anne was casting Thad's cousin some very steamy looks.

That pair needed watching or there would be a surprise bundle arriving nine months from now.

She understood the hot look Malcolm was casting Anne. Hadn't Thad looked at her that way a time or two today?

But Wycke hadn't, at least not that she'd noticed.

She dismissed the thought. Love, not lust, was most important.

She concentrated her attention on Wycke. Had he been a man of poor character, he would have left Thad writhing on the ground with a dislocated arm hanging off his shoulder bone. But he'd stepped forward at once and been quite careful not to hurt him more than necessary to manipulate the bone back in its proper socket. "Truly, my lord. What is it about me that appeals to you?"

He shrugged. "You are elegant and refined."

Thad would be snorting ale through his nose at the remark, and laughing so hard, his sides would split. To Thad, she was a Harpy. How many times had he complained that she was the most vexing lass ever to exist?

"You're a gracious hostess." He tossed her a slightly wicked grin. "Not to mention, you're beautiful. I noticed that from the first. Couldn't stop noticing, truth be told."

Ah, low brain function hard at work.

"So, you found me healthy."

He scratched his head and grinned. "Healthy?" She noticed his eyes dart up and down her body. Discretely, of course. But he'd looked at her chest immediately. Goodness, whoever wrote The Book of Love certainly understood the male animal. "I'd say you are appealing. You're also quite capable of managing a large household. That requires a certain amount of intelligence. You also have a lively wit that I admire."

"Would you and I share a bedchamber if we were to marry?"

His eyes widened and he began to cough in surprise. "Of course not," he blurted. "I wouldn't impose on you...that is... What did you just ask me?"

She shook her head and laughed. "Never mind." She had her answer. Had he truly loved her, he would have wanted her in his bed, wrapped in his arms as they fell asleep. He would have been aching to claim his husbandly rights.

But he had yet to kiss her.

He hadn't even made an attempt to kiss her.

Nor did this task appear to be on his mind.

Perhaps it was, but he hadn't let on. Some men hid their thoughts better than others. Also, his mother and sister were close by. He may not wish to behave like a hound when in their presence.

She understood, but he could have whispered something improper. A request to meet her by the pond at midnight?

Indeed, it seemed Wycke was more in love with the idea of her. Or rather, the idea of having a pretty companion who was raised to be a countess and trained, as he and his sister had been, to make her way comfortably among the elegant *ton*.

Penelope supposed it was a sort of connection between them, a shared culture. One of privilege and duty.

It was something, but not nearly enough for her.

Wycke would never consider making a fool of himself to win her heart. He wasn't besotted with her. She changed the subject, and they proceeded to have a lovely conversation about nothing noteworthy or memorable.

Malcolm, she'd noticed, had disappeared into the copse with Anne on the pretext of chasing tadpoles. Ha! Penelope had done that with Thad when she was younger. Innocently, of course. The only chasing Malcolm intended to do was chase Anne's skirts. No doubt, he intended to crush his lips to Anne's and stick his hands all over her body where they had no right to be, the moment they were out of sight.

She grinned when they emerged from the grove of trees not thirty seconds later, for Anne had a tell-tale blush on her cheeks and her fichu was now in her hand instead of primly covering her bodice.

Malcolm placed Anne's arm in his as he approached them. "Lord Wycke, I'd like a word with ye."

"Oh, Thomas. Please do listen to him," Anne pleaded when her brother frowned.

Wycke glanced at his sister and then at Malcolm. "Not now." By his tone, one got the impression he meant 'not ever'. But Malcolm was having none of it.

"I've asked yer sister to marry me. And now I'm here to ask for yer consent." He stood as tall as an oak tree, his chin tilted upward in pride. "And let me assure ye, I only ask out of politeness because we shall soon be kin. Yer sister loves ye, so I'll be happy to accept ye as my brother. But make no mistake, I'll be marrying Anne with or without yer permission."

"Are all Scots daft?" Wycke turned to glower at the two earls, Caithness and Hume, who were now approaching.

Penelope stood back as the two old men hugged Anne. "Ye'll make a bonnie Caithness bride," Malcolm's granduncle exclaimed, lifting the girl in his arms and twirling her around to mark his consent. He then lifted Lady Wycke and gave her a twirl, although she was no light, little feather.

Hume offered his hearty congratulations.

Penelope did as well, but inside, she was as stunned as Wycke was. Where was the deep and abiding connection? How could the pair know within a matter of hours that they were a perfect match?

Wycke obviously had the same doubts. "MacLauren," he said, folding his arms across his chest. "Let's take this inside. We need to speak privately."

To say matters remained tense was an understatement.

They all returned to the house. The men gathered in Nathaniel's study for the discussion—Wycke, Malcolm, Nathaniel, Beast, and the two Scottish earls were present. But the women were left out.

"Isn't my opinion important?" Anne remarked, her eyes tearing and chin beginning to wobble.

Penelope, Lavinia, Anne, and her mother had gathered in Lavinia's parlor to await the outcome while Poppy, Olivia, and Violet returned to entertain their guests who were still enjoying the day despite the earlier excitement.

Penelope expected more *excitement,* for she knew there could only be one possible result of the men's discussion. Malcolm and Anne would marry, it was only a question of when.

Within the hour, the men strode out of the study.

Malcolm strode straight to Anne. "Yer brother's given his consent."

Anne gasped and turned to her brother with the brightest smile. "Thank you, Thomas."

He nodded, but did not smile back. "However, you will only marry after a six-month courtship. Those are my terms. If you are still determined to go through with this...folly, then you shall have my consent."

Penelope silently scoffed at the notion. Yes, it made sense to have them get to know each other better before entering a lifetime commitment, but those two were not going to wait to get their hands on each other.

If a six-month courtship was required, their little bundle of joy would arrive three months after their marriage. Would anyone be surprised?

The looks that pair tossed each other could light enough fires to keep a town warm during a blizzard.

She wanted to question Wycke about the men's discussion, but knew by his furious expression that he was not going to talk about his sister and that Scottish brute, as he obviously considered Malcolm.

Did he think the same of Thad?

She'd poke him in the nose if he dared utter an unkind remark about him. Thad was *her* Scottish brute and only she could... No, she would never berate Thad again. He was too wonderful. He'd saved her life.

He could call her Loopy all he wished, and it would no longer rile her.

That evening, Wycke sat to her left at supper and the Earl of Hume sat to her right. The Earl of Caithness sat across from her, frowning at her every time she dared converse with Wycke.

Nathaniel was casting her curious glances, no doubt trying to decipher what was on her mind. Goose and Poppy did not look happy. She knew they adored Thad, and wouldn't it be just perfect if Nathaniel and his friends wound up married to Penelope and her friends?

Perhaps.

She glanced at Malcolm and Anne. Oh, they looked like a couple in love. How could they know? Did love at first sight exist?

Penelope picked at the venison on her plate while trying to imagine what marriage to Wycke would be like. Amiable and convenient, certainly.

Marriage to Thad?

Oh, Thad. He had the power to break her heart.

Was it possible he loved her?

Or was he in love with the convenience of having her by his side? Yet, how could it be convenient when she constantly vexed him?

BEFORE HEADING DOWN to breakfast the following morning, Penelope paused by the door of her own bedchamber which was presently occupied by Thad since the doctor had insisted it was safest not to move him.

So many feelings flowed through her, she was almost afraid to see him. But as badly as she wished to avoid him, she was even more desperate to be in his company again.

In truth, she craved it.

Had she any sense, she'd agree to marry Wycke and forget all about the big, muscled ox occupying her bed.

To be precise, the big, muscled Scot who'd taken over her bedchamber, which was the reason she'd spent the night in Lavinia's bedchamber, sharing the right side of her aunt's large bed with Periwinkle, who was not at all happy to have her occupying *his* space.

She'd been jolted awake several times in the wee hours by his sniffing her. *Yes, it's still me. Still occupying your side of Lavinia's bed. Get your wet nose out from under my nightrail.*

Were all males this dense?

Thad certainly was.

His idea of courtship was to fall atop her, tell her she smelled like food, and then ungracefully pass out.

She could not possibly find his actions romantic or endearing.

And yet...this was Thad.

The same man who'd pulled her out of harm's way and taken the full brunt of Monarch's massive hooves to his shoulder. She shuddered, imagining his entire back was now black and blue from the stomping he'd taken while protecting her.

This was the same man who'd ignored his wounds to make certain she was tended to first, which hadn't been necessary since she was unharmed because of his quick actions.

And then he'd consoled Pip.

Oh, heavens! If that big oaf and Pip came down to breakfast wearing matching slings, her entire body would melt into a puddle.

She took a deep breath and willed her hands to stop trembling. "Thad," she said, ridiculously whispering through the door as though her voice would carry through the thick oak. She heard not a sound.

Not a stirring.

As she was debating whether or not to enter, Nathaniel came striding down the hall. He arched an eyebrow and frowned upon noticing her. "What are you doing, Penelope?"

Her chin tipped up and she gave a huff. "It's my bedchamber. Why shouldn't I be in front of it?"

"I don't care that you're in front of it." His frown deepened. "I don't want you inside with my laudanum-crazed friend, who's probably still naked in your bed."

"That's his problem, not mine. Besides, I've already seen him naked. Of course, I was an innocent child at the time, and you, Thad, and Beast were rowdy university boys swimming in nothing but your nature suits in the pond."

"That was almost a decade ago. You stole our clothes. I haven't forgotten." He eyed her warily. "You haven't seen him naked since then, have you?"

"Of course not. If you're going to be so prim about it, then you ought to have given him one of your nightshirts to wear." She turned the latch. "Thad, you'd better cover your hairy—"

"Gad, it's barely past dawn and you're already giving me headaches." Nathaniel placed his hand over hers. "If you go in there, you're coming out betrothed to Thad."

"Don't be ridiculous. I don't intend to climb into bed with him. I just need to fetch a ribbon for my hair."

"I'll see if Poppy has one to spare. I'm sure she has a dozen."

"Hah! Shows what you know about your wife. Poppy doesn't wear ribbons in her hair. She tucks it up with clips and pins which you'd know if you were thinking about anything other than running your hot, little fingers through her unbound hair and… I can't mention the rest. It's too lewd."

Nathaniel threw up his hands and grunted in dismay. "Fine, go in. But if you do, you're marrying him. Double wedding. Malcolm and Anne. You and Thad."

"Hah!"

"Wycke and I will be right behind you, toting rifles pointed at those big Scots...and sacks of ammunition, although I doubt either of them will need much convincing. Not with loaded weapons aimed at their heads."

She was spared the need of a response when Thad suddenly opened the door. He was washed and fully dressed, obviously having had assistance. His arm was resting in a sling and he appeared to be in pain still, for lines of strain were etched into his handsome face.

His eyes had a sleepy tilt to them.

They were dark and hooded and steamy.

Those wicked little butterflies in Penelope's stomach began to rouse and flutter yet again.

"Greville helped me," Thad explained, noting her gaping mouth and grinning in response to her look of confusion. "Thank ye for sending him to me, Nathaniel." He tucked a finger under her chin to close her mouth. "I'm feeling much better this morning. I'll be off to meet my regiment right after breakfast and bring them here. We'll camp along the stream behind Gosling Hall. I'll be out of yer bedchamber within the hour, Loopy. Sorry about...falling on ye...and the rest of it."

She sighed. "Stay as long as you need. Periwinkle and I have become quite cozy. He's sniffed me thoroughly."

Thad assumed this meant he had permission to sniff her, too. "Och, always delicious. Ye smell like a–"

"Don't you dare say it, you lout!"

"–sausage patty."

She wanted to strike him, but she wasn't that cruel. He was too badly injured and even the lightest touch would have brought him to his knees, writhing in pain.

Nathaniel groaned and turned to walk off. "I'll see you both downstairs." But before he strode off, he mouthed the word 'marry' as though threatening her with a betrothal to Thad if she didn't behave.

She and Thad never behaved around each other.

Why was this a surprise to her brother?

Her gaze mellowed as she returned her attention to Thad. He had been injured saving her life and she would never forget his bravery.

She blushed under the force of his stare.

She stared back at him. Oh, he was big and magnificent. And he'd dressed in typical Thad fashion, which meant completely out of fashion. Once again, he'd neglected to don his vest, cravat, and jacket, so all she could see was the vast expanse of his elegant, white lawn shirt that hugged his rock-hard arms and broad chest.

But she also noticed a bit of red leather peeking out from the sling used to hold his arm in place, and realized he'd taken The Book of Love for himself.

"Is there a reason ye were standing outside my door?" he asked.

"It's *my* door."

He grinned at her. "Verra well, lass. Is there a reason–"

"Ribbon." She glanced down at herself. "I needed a sunflower yellow one to match my gown." The fabric itself was a plain white dimity but trimmed in yellow silk at the edge of the sleeves and had a belt of matching yellow silk that circled her body just beneath her bosom. "Is there a reason you're stealing that book from me?"

He rolled his eyes. "I'm reading it, lass. I won't ride off with it, if that's what concerns ye. What the author has to say is quite interesting. I read much of it last night."

"Oh, really? About the male lower brain and higher brain? Or did you not get beyond the lower brain function? Is this why you keep staring at my chest? Stop looking *there*. I'd appreciate it if you looked at my face. My body is no concern of yours. I refuse to be regarded as the fertile vessel into which to spill your seed."

"Don't talk about yerself like that, Loopy. Ye know ye're not that to me." He glanced at the book, then withdrew it and handed it to her.

"Ye ought to be the one reading it. Then ye might understand what you mean to me."

She took it grudgingly. "Oh, is that so? Then pray tell me, what am I to you?"

"Everything," he said quietly.

She opened her mouth to toss back an indignant retort, but could find no words. She stood before him like a fool, her lungs filling with air. An eternity passed between them. Finally, she found her voice. "What did you just say?"

"Ye heard me, lass."

She let out the breath she'd been holding. "Thad, do you mean it?"

"I'm looking at all of ye. Don't expect me to pretend I'm not lusting after yer glorious body. But it's yer heart I'm truly after." He took a step closer. "I may have gone about it badly."

"You think so?"

It was impossible to overlook her sarcasm. "Fine, I went about it all wrong. But I never considered proposing to anyone else."

"Thad," she said with an ache to her voice. "You haven't proposed to me."

Lying to his kinsmen about their betrothal was not the same as declaring himself to her.

He appeared startled, but then he nodded. "I'll tell ye now."

Her eyebrows shot up. "Tell me? You think you're going to *tell* me what to do?"

"Blessed saints! Can ye for once not twist my words? I'm trying to ask ye to marry me."

"While we're standing in the hallway?"

"Is this not romantic enough for ye? Well, that's too bad, lass. I may now be in line to inherit an earldom, but I'm still me. I won't be donning silk breeches or powdered wigs. I won't be reciting sonnets to yer beauty. Nor will I be asking ye again. Ye have my offer. Mull it over. When ye're ready, give me an answer. But don't take too long, for Caithness and Hume are not patient men. Nor is Castlereagh." He started to walk away, then turned back. "Nor am I."

He stalked down the hall.

She wanted to call him back, but her pride would not allow it. "You big, dumb Scot," she muttered under her breath, entering her bedchamber to retrieve the ribbon that seemed inconsequential now. "I will not marry you to save your cowardly hide. I never want to see you again, Thaddius MacLauren."

She withdrew the ribbon from the drawer in her vanity, then peered in the mirror while she wound it neatly through her chignon. "Looks ridiculous." She removed the clips and ribbon, hastily running her fingers through her curls as they tumbled around her shoulders and down her back.

She was about to start again when she sensed someone standing at her door.

Thad was back, filling the doorway with his broad shoulders.

He was frowning.

Was he taking back his proposal?

"I'm still in pain, Loopy. I had a wretched night's sleep. Will you forgive me for behaving like an arse just now?"

She sighed. "If you forgive me. I also spent an uncomfortable night. Periwinkle was…" She shook her head and laughed. "I'm never sleeping with that pampered dog again. Thad, you shouldn't be riding out this morning if you're still in pain. It can't be good for your shoulder."

"I'll be all right." He cast her an endearingly boyish grin. "Ye look beautiful, lass. I would recite sonnets to yer beauty, if I knew any. Ye should leave yer hair like that. But I didn't return to talk about yer hair or ribbons or poems."

"Why did you come back?"

"Because of something I neglected to do yesterday." He strode forward and drew her into his embrace using his good arm. "This."

He crushed his mouth to hers, taking advantage that her lips were parted in surprise to gain entrance and give her a highly improper kiss that was unexpectedly gentle, and at the same time, typically impudent. For this was Thad, always filled with Scottish arrogance and unspoken challenge, and yet divinely tender and heartfelt.

She leaned into his big, solidly muscled body, absorbing his heat and strength. He was tall, and the top of her head barely reached his shoulder. They shouldn't have fit so perfectly together, but they did. His kiss was possessive, and yet it did not feel as though he was merely claiming her, but offering a piece of himself in return. In this moment, she wanted all of him.

She could have him, too.

All she needed to do was to accept his marriage proposal, but that would mean turning her heart over to him and trusting that he would never break it.

He held such power over her, it frightened her.

She carefully slid her arm up his chest, her palm tingling beneath the corded tension of his body. *Heaven help me, he feels so good.*

He teased his tongue along her lower lip, and then slid it between her lips in a slow and sensual mating dance with her tongue.

Oh, yes.

The big Scot knew how to kiss her proper.

Her eyes had closed the moment their mouths touched, allowing her to run through each sensation she'd read in The Book of Love. His touch, fiery. The taste of him, hot and delicious.

She moaned against his mouth.

"Loopy, I dinna want to let ye go." Oh, the rugged sweetness of his deep, rumbling brogue.

She kissed the freshly shaven line of his jaw, inhaling his scent of lather and musk.

She drew back as he loosened his grip on her body and her eyes flitted open. She gasped, for what she saw in Thad's eyes was raw, savage desire.

He dropped his hand to his side, and then turned away. "Wait for me, lass. We'll talk when I return."

He strode off.

He'd return later in the day with his regiment.

She wanted to follow him out, but couldn't. Her entire body was limp and her legs felt buttery. Her hands shook and her heart beat so fast, she feared to swoon. The notion was ridiculous. Swoon over Thad?

Lord Wycke had proposed to her as well. She'd put him off, promising him an answer by tomorrow evening.

She had a choice to make. Would she choose the amiable earl who offered her security and a comfortable home close to her family and friends in the Cotswolds? Or the impossibly provoking Highlander who might someday be an earl and would expect her to live with him in Scotland?

What was she going to do?

CHAPTER ELEVEN

THAD WAS IN monumental pain by the time he, Malcolm, and Robbie returned to Wellesford in the afternoon with their regiment. Nathaniel and Beast rode out to greet them and help them settle their men in the field behind Gosling Hall.

Hume and Caithness were not far behind.

Despite having to prepare for another elegant party this evening, Poppy and Penelope, and an army of Sherbourne servants carting food, ale, and other supplies, soon followed. Goose was beside them with her own servants from Gosling Hall, bringing down more food and useful wares.

Thad felt everyone's gaze on him, their prying eyes following his every movement with concern. However, he refused to show weakness or admit he was in agony.

He groaned inwardly as Penelope approached, looking ready to drag him by the ear to Sherbourne Manor and toss him into bed. Not with her, of course. Alone. Because he was injured and had overdone it. "Bollocks, lass. Don't tell me what I should or should not be doing. These are my men."

"I see. So you feel it is important to make a fool of yourself in front of them when you faint."

He grumbled. "Men don't faint."

To his relief, she rolled her eyes and laughed. "You are the stubbornest man who ever lived. *When* you collapse in your manly fashion,

I shall merely stand by and watch you topple. Indeed, I think I will sell tickets for the event and take wagers on when it will happen."

"Lass, ye're cruel." But he grinned at her, for she looked soft and sweet, and she was right. He was not steady on his feet and his shoulder was throbbing.

"There's a tray of scones and a pot of tea waiting for us under the shade tree by the stream. Surely, your men won't mind if you spend a few minutes with the sister of one of your hosts. Indeed, they would believe you to be quite rude if you refused my request."

He arched an eyebrow. "Ye're manipulating me."

"Yes, but in a nice way. Oh, Thad, please. I'm so worried about you. How could you not have felt a jolt through your bones with every stride your horse took? That has to be wearing on your body. Even if you are a big ox."

"Ah, there's the Loopy I know and..." He was going to say 'love' but stopped himself. He wasn't certain how she felt about him. Yes, she cared for him. How much?

Fortunately, she did not give him grief about his comment. "Sit down. Look, even your men are taking a moment to relax and eat. You aren't the only one in need of a little respite."

She was right. It wouldn't do him any harm. The tents had now been set up and the horses tended to, so sitting down to a hearty meal was decidedly in order. Poppy and Goose, with several of their servants, were helping those too injured to manage on their own.

Out of the corner of his eye, he noticed a few of the men preparing to strip out of their uniforms and jump in the stream. "I'll sit with ye, lass. But ye'd better look this way."

"Why?" she asked and turned to follow his gaze. "Oh!"

A blush ran up her cheeks, and she began to fuss with the teapot, trying to pour him a cup, but her hands were shaking. A little of it spilled onto the tray. "You might have explained why I should not look and spared me the sight of..."

He chuckled. "Ye've seen naked men before. Ye've seen me, for certain. Blink all ye want, lass. Ye canno' get rid of the memory by washing it out of yer eyes like a stray eyelash."

"Oh, Thad. Don't tease me. I was so worried about you."

He placed his hand over hers. "I know. I appreciate it more than I can say. But I'm still a stubborn arse. These are my men. I canno' leave them before I see them all safely returned home."

"I know it's important to you. But you won't last through the journey if you push yourself too hard now. Walk me back to the house. Rest a few hours before our party. No one will notice your absence. Even if they do, they'll see you've walked off with me. Let them imagine whatever they wish." She made no move to draw her hand away, so he continued to hold it. "Please, Thad. Do it for me."

"Verra well. For ye, Loopy." He glanced at the tray. "Are those raisin scones?"

She nodded. "Of course."

"Och, lass. Thank ye. Do ye mind if we eat before I walk ye back to the house?"

She bestowed him with a brilliant smile. "I'd never deprive you of your favorite treat."

In truth, she was his treat. Every moment he spent with Penelope felt like a slice of heaven. The sun was shining. A soft breeze wafted through the trees and ruffled her auburn hair.

The scones were delicious and so was her smile. He wanted to tell her that he loved her, but her smile faded into a frown at the very moment he mustered the resolve. "What's the matter?"

She sighed. "Thad, I'm so puzzled."

"About what?" He set down his cup of tea, prepared to listen.

"Malcolm and Anne. How have they made the strong connections necessary for a lasting love?"

He shook his head and sighed. "Och, lass. The Book of Love is not gospel. It canno' cover every reason why a couple might decide they suit. And who's to say that the passionate feelings Malcolm and Anne have for each other will last? They've leaped into their decision. I hope it will prove to be a happy one, but it's far from certain."

"So do I. It seems right that love should win out. I hope it will work for them. Anne is a lovely girl. But what an odd pairing they are."

He nodded in agreement. "Aye, but also sensible in many ways. Malcolm's been given the order as well. Find a Sassenach wife. He's been raised to be Caithness's successor and takes his responsibility very seriously. So his brain has already adjusted to his sense of duty. He's been around women, perhaps not in a while since we were all off fighting Napoleon, but he is no young fool. He knows the sort of woman he wants."

"But he barely knows Anne."

He shrugged. "She's young and pretty. She's an earl's sister. Unmarried. She fits most of the requirements on his list."

"Love isn't about making lists." She began to nibble her lip. "Shouldn't it be something more?"

"For certain. But we aren't all given the time we need to make a proper decision. My cousin is a good man. He won't be easily led astray by a pretty smile, or other parts of a woman's body, for that matter. But if I know Malcolm, he saw much more in Anne than...a healthy chest." He cleared his throat, for it had suddenly turned taut and ragged. "He saw acceptance in her eyes when she looked at him. He saw admiration and wonder, as well. To her, he wasn't a mere title to be claimed. He wasn't a big Scottish oaf to be used to gain stature. He was handsome in her eyes. He was clever and valiant in her eyes."

He noticed Loopy's own eyes begin to glisten.

"Lass, that's what I hope ye see when ye look at me. Perhaps in time, ye'll come to feel this way about me. I know I'm no prize."

"Thad," she whispered with an ache to her voice. "I'm so sorry I was ever cruel to you. You are the best. I never meant for you to think otherwise. I'm the one with the Harpy tongue. How can you possibly care for me?"

He ran a hand through his hair, uncertain how to answer. Perhaps the best way was to show her. "My regiment will be here for one more day. We have the dinner party tonight, so I doubt you and I will have much time to speak quietly. But I'd like ye to meet me by the pond after breakfast tomorrow. Bring The Book of Love with ye."

She tipped her head in confusion. "What are you going to show me that I haven't already learned from this book?"

He reached out and ran his thumb gently across her lower lip. "Och, lass," he said in a ragged whisper, "I think it's time ye learned about my heart."

To Penelope's relief, Thad returned to Sherbourne Manor without protest after washing down his scones. His men were well settled and receiving the best care. The Earl of Caithness, Malcolm, and Robbie were there to attend to any regimental issues, and the Sherbourne and Gosling staffs were busy attending to all other matters. "I've asked Dr. Carmichael to look in on you once he's finished with the injured."

"It is no'–"

"He's going to tend to you for *my* peace of mind," she insisted. Although he tried to hide it, she saw that he had a slight limp and he couldn't seem to move his left arm without difficulty, which was not surprising since the impact had pushed it out of its socket just yesterday. She accompanied him into the house and upstairs. "We haven't moved you out of my bedchamber. I'll be cuddling with Periwinkle for another night."

"Lass, I'm sorry. It isn't necessary. Our tents are set up. I can sleep in one of them by the stream. It is no hardship for me."

"You have a long ride ahead of you, Thad. Let Dr. Carmichael examine your wounds to be certain there isn't something more to worry about. I need to know you'll heal. After all, you were injured because of me. I'll never forgive myself if I've done you permanent harm."

He frowned. "It wasn't yer fault. I don't ever want to hear ye casting blame on yerself. If ye must cast blame on someone...or something...then do it on that damn garden snake or skittish colt. Blessed saints! I would no' ever forgive myself if you had come to harm."

They reached her bedchamber, and she would have marched in along with him had he not stopped in the doorway to block her. "This is as far as ye go, lass. Do ye need anything from in here?"

You.

Of course, suggesting such a thing was out of the question. "No, I'm fine for now. Greville will help you out of your clothes. I'll have a tub brought up. Soak in the hot water for a while. I think it will help to relax your stiff muscles."

His gaze upon her softened. "I'll do that, lass."

Oh, goodness. He had a way of looking at her that was at once tender and steamy. She cleared her throat. Fiery, too.

The butterflies in her stomach were in their usual fluttering frenzy.

"I'll stop by later," she said in a breathless whisper and hurried away to order his bath and seek out Greville. Thad would never be able to pull off his boots by himself, but he was stubborn enough to try and further damage his shoulder.

After finishing those small errands, she intended to return to the regimental camp, but paused when she noticed Malcolm and Anne in each other's arms in a corner of the parlor. What was it they saw in each other?

When Malcolm drew away and returned to the camp, Penelope took the opportunity to approach Anne.

"Good afternoon, Penelope. Is something amiss?" The girl glowed, there was no other way to explain the light in her eyes and happiness in her expression. "Other than my cautious brother being furious with my decision?"

"Captain MacLauren," Penelope said, referring to Thad, "thinks quite highly of his cousin. But I must admit to being as surprised as your brother. What made you accept a man you've known for less than a day?"

They settled on the settee, Anne obviously eager to speak her mind. Thad had given his opinion earlier, but Penelope was curious and wanted it confirmed by Anne.

Anne placed a hand over her heart. "I'm not certain I can explain this feeling. Yes, we've only just met, and there's no denying there's a physical aspect to his appeal," she said with a blush. "He's big and muscled, and his scent is divine. And who can resist that deep, rumbling brogue? Besides being handsome as sin, he's kind and protective. Most important, I trust him. Even though we've only known each other a very short time, I feel as though I've known him forever. I suppose that makes no sense."

"Coming to this conclusion within a matter of hours doesn't, but when does one's heart ever follow a sensible course?" She debated whether to confide in Anne about The Book of Love, and ultimately decided against it. First, Anne seemed instinctively to understand about the five senses, having described the look, scent, and sound of Malcolm as reasons for her attraction. Of course, there was no doubt she'd also enjoyed his touch and the taste of his kiss. "Anne, do you have no qualms about leaving your family?"

"I've been trained to take over the role of lady of the manor since birth. I expect you have been as well." Her effervescent smile dimmed a little. "But yes, leaving my loved ones is the only thing to dampen my joy. Malcolm has already told me that my mother may live with us if that is my wish. He has great respect for the elders. How can I not love such a man?"

Penelope sighed, realizing she was the dense one. "Does it not trouble you that you'll be living in the Highlands?" Indeed, Caithness was considered far north even for a Highlander.

"Far from the London whirl?" She shook her head and smiled. "I've never appreciated the assemblies, balls, and other elegant entertainments offered in town. My brother enjoys this fast life, but I never have. Living in the Highlands will be no sacrifice for me."

"I see. Do you mind if we speak of your brother?"

"What is it you wish to know about Thomas? He's been very good to me and my mother."

Penelope nodded. "He reminds me of my own brother. Nathaniel has always been a family man, quite protective of those he loves. He's serious about his duties and obligations. My impression is your brother is the same."

Anne shook her head and laughed. "Oh, Thomas is not usually so serious. Of course, he's attentive to his duties and quite honorable. But he's been on his best behavior around you. He's hardly the saint he'd like you to believe. At university, he earned the name of Wicked Wycke, although I don't believe he was ever truly wicked."

Penelope was surprised, for Thomas Halford hadn't come across as anything other than kind and sincere.

"He's a good man," Anne assured her. "But he's suddenly got it into his head that he must marry before the Season is out."

"Why?"

"Who's to say? Perhaps my mother's pleas finally wore him down. Perhaps he simply felt it was time to move forward."

What Anne did not say was most important. She did not say that he'd met the woman of his dreams. Wycke's heart was not the motivation for his decision. Penelope ought to have been devastated, or at the least, overset. She was neither, simply relieved. "Thank you, Anne. I appreciate our little talk."

"Me, too." She cast Penelope a gracious smile, but caught her hand before she had the chance to move away. "Penelope, you have been most kind to me and my family. So please do not take offense at what I am about to say."

"Go on. I'm listening." She suddenly wondered whether she'd underestimated Wycke's sister. That she was shy and quiet did not mean she was dull-witted. Poppy was similarly reserved, but she was the smartest of all of them.

"You know the way I look at Malcolm. Indeed, it's shocked quite everyone, except for Malcolm and me."

Penelope nodded.

"This is the way I hope my brother will feel about the woman he'll marry. Completely besotted and heart soaring whenever she is near. As important, it is the way I wish his betrothed to feel about him. However, I don't sense anything like this in either my brother or you. All I see between the pair of you is level-headed reason. Respect and friendship, yes. Shouldn't there be something more?" She took a deep breath and continued. "I have the utmost regard for you, Penelope. I wish you and Thomas were a match, but I don't see how you are."

"It is something I've given serious thought to, as well." After assuring Anne she had not taken offense, Penelope left her to go in search of Dr. Carmichael. She wanted to make certain he hadn't forgotten to stop by her bedchamber to examine Thad before returning to his infirmary.

Wycke called to her as she left the house through the music room doors and started across the garden along the back path to Gosling Hall. Normally, she would have gone out the front door and crossed the meadow separating the two stately houses, but taking this route toward the back gate was the quickest way to the stream where the soldiers were camped.

"Is there something I can do for you, my lord? I wish to make certain the doctor doesn't leave before looking in on Captain MacLauren."

He gave a wry laugh. "My sister is about to elope to the Highlands with a complete stranger and," he cast her a look up and down, "the woman I hope to marry seems about to do the same."

He appeared more confused than hurt or unhappy.

She sighed. "Lord Wycke, I–"

"Please call me Thomas. May I call you Penelope? It may seem foolish to you since I sense you are about to turn me down for Captain MacLauren."

"Not at all foolish. I hope we shall become good friends." She blushed lightly. "We would be family if your sister marries Malcolm MacLauren and I..." Her voice trailed off. She couldn't quite bring herself to admit she would marry Thad.

She had no doubt of her affection for the big Scot, of course. Hadn't she always loved him? Only now, it had matured into something deep and abiding. These feeling threatened to swallow her whole. He'd claimed her heart. He'd claimed all of her, body and soul. What she did not yet trust was Thad's feelings for her.

Yes, he loved her.

But was it in the same soul-searing way she loved him? He did seem to want physical contact with her. But he'd never properly courted her, merely blurted to his kinsmen that she was the one for him when his back was up against the wall. So, was he now convincing himself he'd made the right decision? Willing himself to feel more than he did?

"Penelope, I wish you every happiness. But I hope you will decide to find that happiness with me." She was surprised and jolted out of her thoughts when Thomas took her into his arms and gave her a hug. "My family and I will leave tomorrow. I know the regiment leaves the day after that, but I'm eager to separate Anne from Malcolm before something dire happens. I must douse that fire before it burns out of control. However, I wish to thank you sincerely for your hospitality."

"They are a combustible pair, aren't they?" Penelope laughed.

"Anne's greatest wish is that you find the girl who sets your heart afire like that."

"Perhaps if I were young and foolish, I might act impulsively. But in my position, how can I risk it? Besides, these intense fires quickly die out. No, I'd much rather keep my eyes open and head clear. I know quality when I see it and you are that. Give me a chance to prove that you and I are a good fit." He gave her another quick embrace before returning to the house.

Penelope continued to Gosling Hall, her mind in even more of a whirl. Lord Wycke's comments made sense. Even The Book of Love spoke of the different stages of love. A mature love was one that would last. Once the burning desire died out, something deeper and more meaningful had to replace it or else the husband and wife were left with nothing but ashes.

Still, didn't the couple have to start out with some interest to bind them together? If she refused Wycke's suit, would his heart break?

She doubted it.

As she crossed the garden, she glanced back and looked up toward her bedchamber window, merely wondering what Thad was doing now. Her heart gave a little hitch. He was standing by the window, wearing no shirt as he looked down on her.

Her heart hitched again.

She tried to avert her gaze, but couldn't.

Where was his shirt? Could that big, Scottish oaf not find one to wear? And why was he staring at her with his arms crossed and frowning? With his bad arm, didn't that hurt?

Oh, dear!

Had he mistaken the reason for Wycke's embrace?

How much had he seen?

And was it too much to ask for him to put on clothes if he was going to stand there and scowl at her?

More important, did he not trust her?

How could he claim to love her if he had no faith in her?

CHAPTER TWELVE

"THIS IS NOT at all proper," Dr. Carmichael muttered when Penelope insisted on accompanying him to her bedchamber now occupied by Thad who, she hoped, had put on clothes by now.

Not that she would have minded seeing more of him, but not in the doctor's presence.

"It is *my* bedchamber. You and my brother's valet, Greville, will be present to vouch that nothing untoward happens. Please do not attempt to stop me, Doctor. I need to see the damage to his shoulder for myself because Captain MacLauren will lie to me and tell me he's fine when I know he isn't."

"I could simply report my findings to you after I've examined him."

"It won't do." She tipped her head up and cast him an indignant look. "You know he needs to be scolded into taking care of himself. I can do this better than anyone. Why do you think he calls me a Harpy? We must stop him from doing something foolish, which he'll certainly do unless he's made to rest. How else will he properly heal?"

The doctor ran a hand roughly across the nape of his neck. "I still don't think it's wise."

What a bother. She'd forgotten Angus Carmichael was a stubborn Scot himself. Were they all hardheaded louts? "I've been duly warned and scolded. I'm still going in."

She was also the sister of the present earl and knew the doctor was not going to challenge her authority in her own home. He frowned at her when they reached her bedchamber door, his obvious displeasure a final attempt to have her see reason and not barge in on Thad.

When he realized he couldn't shake her determination, he sighed and knocked on the door. "Captain MacLauren, you have company. May we come in?"

Greville opened the door, his eyes bulging when Penelope strode in behind the doctor. "Lady Penelope! His lordship is undressed."

Thad was seated on the bed, wearing nothing but a towel loosely tucked around his waist, his rock-hard muscles on display. "Bollocks, lass! Ye canno' be in here." He rose, no doubt intending to bodily push her out, and then realized he had nothing on under his towel, so he turned to look for something to put on.

That's when she saw the extent of the damage to his back and shoulder. "Thad!"

He realized where she'd been looking and groaned. "Dinna make too much of it."

Her hands fisted. "You deserve a good smack about the head, you big ox."

"What did I do now?"

"Your entire back is black and blue. Your skin is torn where Monarch's hooves fell on you." She shot him an accusatory glower. "You should have remained in bed all day to heal. What possessed you to ride out? There were others able to collect your regiment and bring them to Sherbourne Manor. You're fortunate you didn't fall off your horse. How could you be so reckless? Knowing your injuries?"

She wanted to cry, for he had to be in agonizing pain. "Oh, Thad. Sit down and let the doctor tend to your wounds." She turned to Dr. Carmichael. "What can I do to help?"

"Leave," he and Thad said at once.

She ignored them. "Besides that."

She turned to Thad again. In truth, she couldn't stop looking at him. He was big and beautifully muscled, so magnificently sculpted against his warm skin. She made the mistake of touching him. Instantly, her heart began to flutter and her legs turned to butter.

She wanted to kiss her way up and down his body.

Taste him.

She shook out of the enticing notion, but did not remove her gaze from him. His shoulders were broad and his stomach was finely honed and lean. Everything about him exuded power and strength. His legs were long and nicely shaped from what she could see of them, for the towel covered them to his knees.

But the rest of him from the waist up was open to her view, and she was soaking all of him in.

Blessed Mother.

Who suddenly turned up the heat in here?

It felt like a thousand fires blazing.

But there wasn't so much as a twig lit in the hearth.

She tore her gaze from his body and studied his face. His hair was wet from his recent bath and brushed off his brow. No doubt, he'd run his fingers casually through that thick mane of his to put some order to it.

His skin was a sun-kissed golden and he smelled like sandalwood soap.

Lord, lord, lord. Did a finer looking man exist?

"Och, lass. Will ye no' go away?" Thad scowled at her when she sat beside him on the bed.

"No, I will not. I wish to hear what Dr. Carmichael tells you." She turned to the doctor who appeared decidedly uncomfortable, as did Greville. Perhaps she should not have plunked herself down on the counterpane beside Thad, seeing as he was clutching the ends of his towel to make certain it did not slip off him. "I will not have you lie to me and tell me all is fine when I can see that it isn't."

"Go away, lass," he repeated. "Yer betrothed will no' be pleased to find ye here with me."

Her eyes rounded in surprise. "I knew it. You were spying on me."

He groaned lightly. "I was merely gazing out the window when I saw you run into Wycke's arms."

"That's really why you're scowling at me." She shook her head and laughed. "Thaddius MacLauren, you are without a doubt the biggest fool who ever lived. I did not run into his arms and you know it. He pulled me into them. If you must know, he told me he was leaving tomorrow. He only embraced me to thank me for my hospitality and wish me well."

Instead of replying, he yelped as Dr. Carmichael touched his shoulder to check on the damage.

Penelope cast him an accusatory look. "That hurt you, didn't it?"

He frowned back. "No."

"Fine, then you won't mind if I press down on the same spot."

He jumped up, his towel fortunately still secure about his waist, although it had fallen a little lower and was hanging on his hips, if one wanted to be precise about it. Would she burn in the eternal fires of Hell if she wished for that towel to slide off his powerfully built, warrior body? "Loopy, enough of this nonsense. Get out."

She rose to stand beside him, trying her best not to breathe in the scent of sandalwood and his male heat. "Not until we strike a bargain."

Before Thad had a chance to accept or refuse, she turned to Greville. "Take all his clothes out of my bedchamber. He's to remain in here for the rest of the day. Tomorrow if necessary, as well."

"Move a muscle, Greville, and I will shoot ye. I will no' be treated like a child. Set out my clothes, if ye wish to be of help, for I'll be joining everyone for supper." He arched an eyebrow, obviously daring Penelope to contradict his intentions. "Tomorrow, my regiment plans to march through Wellesford, and I intend to be among their ranks."

She eyed him warily. "No one told me anything about this."

"Because it isn't any of yer business, lass. It's a parade to thank the citizens of Wellesford for their assistance. There'll be pipers and drummers, and we'll all be dressed in our clan tartans." He cast her a wicked grin. "Ye would no' wish to deprive the female population of me in my kilt, would ye?"

She meant to be stern, but laughed instead. "Do as you wish, you stubborn Scot. You'll do it anyway."

He emitted a hearty chuckle. "Now that's the pot calling the kettle black." But he took her hand when she raised it in surrender and began to turn away. "I'll strike a bargain with ye, lass. I'll march in the parade, but I want ye to march beside me. I'll need something soft to break my fall should I stumble."

She could have shot back a smart retort, for he was obviously goading her. Yet he wanted her beside him, and this was his ridiculously backhanded way of asking her. She decided to be serious for a moment. "Thad, you know I'll always look out for you."

"Aye," he said with a tender ache to his rumbling brogue, "ye always have." He kept hold of her hand. "Did ye mean it when ye said Wycke was merely bidding ye farewell?"

"Yes."

"So, he isn't staying?"

"He and his family leave first thing in the morning."

He glanced at Greville and the doctor, then just shook his head and sighed. "Did ye give him an answer to his marriage proposal?"

She shook her head. "No. He didn't press me for one and we didn't discuss it." She glanced at the doctor and Greville who had to be listening intently even though they were turned away and trying to appear busy, the doctor by fumbling through his medical bag and Greville by fussing with Thad's clothes. "I'll tell you about it tomorrow morning at the pond. We're still meeting there, aren't we?"

"Aye, lass. I haven't forgotten."

She slipped her hand out of his and left the room to go in search of Olivia and Poppy. They'd been friends for as long as she could remember, and she'd always discussed her innermost thoughts and fears with them.

Now, she needed them more than ever.

She wanted to accept Thad's offer of marriage, but couldn't bring herself to do it until she was certain of his motives for marrying her. Or was she setting an impossibly high standard for him to meet by holding out for utter, complete, and soul-searing love?

She and Thad knew each other too well for their fiery heat, assuming he had any burning feelings for her, to turn to mere ashes. Their connections ran deep.

But they also constantly goaded and prodded each other, often behaving like children. And yet, when it mattered, they looked out for each other. Did this not count for something?

She hoped her friends would help her find the answer she sought.

As she approached the regimental camp, she happened to see Poppy and Nathaniel sharing a quiet moment under one of the shade trees by the stream.

She saw the way Nathaniel was looking at Poppy, the love reflected in his eyes as he gazed at her, seeming to soak all of her in. He took her hands in his and held them gently. He shifted his body toward her, as though pulled closer by an irresistible force. Poppy had a similar glow in her eyes, a reflection of the love she held for him. She eased closer, drawn to him by this same force that had drawn him toward her. It was as though the world had fallen away and no one else existed for these two.

Having no wish to disturb them in their private moment, Penelope turned away to seek out Olivia. She saw her friend standing with Beast beside one of the tents. But as she approached, she realized Olivia and Beast were also sharing a moment.

Suddenly, she felt like an intruder.

But watching Beast, this fearsome and powerful duke, caress Olivia's cheek with an open and tender look of longing, seemed to help her find the answers she sought. Not that she actually had her answers, but she now understood what to look for.

Oh, she'd read The Book of Love, but hadn't allowed herself to fully experience each sensation. Thad had kissed her, given her a first kiss she'd never forget. She'd called it a test and used him as her test frog, but she was through *using* him. It was time for her to trust him, to offer her heart to him. To finally be honest with herself and accept that as hard as it would be to leave her friends and family, it would be devastating never to see Thad again.

And who else would she marry, if not Thad?

She loved him to the depths of her soul and could not bring herself to allow any other man to touch her body. Not even Thomas Halford, Earl of Wycke, who was handsome and kind and would probably be a dutiful husband, but how could she ever share his bed when her thoughts would always be on that big Scot who'd saved her life?

Her heart was still lodged in her throat just thinking of Thad in that towel and how badly she'd wanted it to slip off him.

Goodness, she was depraved.

That evening, while dressing in Lavinia's quarters, and although Emily had earlier fetched the sea-blue, silk gown and matching slippers, gloves and undergarments, she'd planned to wear for tonight's supper, she realized Emily had neglected to choose a necklace to go along with her attire.

"I'll be right back," Penelope said once Emily had laced her into her gown. She'd waited for just the right moment to make her quick exit, knowing the girl was now occupied, attempting to clasp a pearl brooch onto Periwinkle's collar.

Of course, Periwinkle's brooch matched the one Lavinia intended to wear this evening.

Penelope adored her aunt, but her insistence on having Periwinkle's collar match whichever necklace she happened to be wearing was a bit much, even for poor Periwinkle who did not look at all pleased.

He barked and darted away every time Emily tried to clip his collar on him. "Oh, you're such a bad boy," Emily muttered in frustration.

"Good boy," Penelope whispered, encouraging him to misbehave.

With Lavinia and Emily distracted, she slipped out the door and made her way down the hall to her bedchamber. She wanted to simply walk in, but she hadn't lost her mind completely, at least not yet.

She knocked instead. "Thad, are you decent? May I come in?"

No response.

She knocked again. "Thad?"

Perhaps he'd gone downstairs already, or so she convinced herself and opened the door since no one was lingering in the hallway to stop her. The shades in her bedchamber had not been drawn, allowing the last rays of sunlight to filter in and cast just enough light for her to make out the outline of Thad's body in her bed.

He was turned away from her, his weight settled on his good shoulder as he slept. The counterpane was twisted around his bare torso, covering his midsection and curling downward like a vine around Thad's long legs. His upper body was exposed, and her heart ached to see the massive spread of black and blue, not to mention the torn flesh, across his injured shoulder.

She forgot about retrieving her necklace, and instead, tiptoed to the other side of the bed for a glimpse of his face as he slept. Dr. Carmichael must have given him a hefty dose of laudanum to quell his pain, otherwise Thad would have been glaring at her and ordering her to go away.

And because he was a thickheaded Scot, had he not been rendered unconscious, he would likely have insisted on dressing, determined to come down to supper even though he was in no shape to do it.

Thankfully, he was sleeping soundly.

She heard his soft breaths and saw the gentle rise and fall of his chest.

Unable to help herself, she reached out to gently brush back a stray lock that had curled on his damp brow.

"Are you developing a fever?" she whispered, frowning.

She hadn't put on her gloves, not needing them to merely enter her chamber and select a necklace. So, she ran her hand lightly along his neck and down his body, her fingers tingling as she brushed them along the light spray of auburn hair on his chest.

Most Scots had pasty-white complexions and their skin burned easily in the sun. But Thad's skin was lightly tanned. She ran her hand along his muscled arm and frowned. He was overly warm, and his skin was damp, not only his forehead, which was worrisome enough.

She rose and crossed to her bureau to retrieve one of her handkerchiefs. She always kept a basin and ewer of water on her bureau, so she poured a little of the water onto her handkerchief and wrung out just enough moisture so as not to soak Thad when she wiped it across his brow and along his neck to cool him down.

Sitting beside him once more, she leaned close to better dab his forehead. Then she wiped the wet handkerchief lightly along his neck. She leaned closer, for he still smelled clean from his earlier bath and the sandalwood scent drew her to him like a moth to a flame.

Thad shifted slightly and his eyes flickered open. "Lass, am I dreaming? Is it really you?"

"It's me."

He emitted a sexy growl and nudged her down beside him. Before she had the chance to protest, he rolled over her, propping on his good elbow to ease the weight of his big body off her. "I must be dreaming. Ye look beautiful. Ye always do. I'm going to kiss you."

Once again, she had no chance to protest before he closed his mouth over hers, his lips warm and demanding. They felt rough and dry as they crushed against her mouth, but she knew it was the fault of the laudanum and not because of any lack in his magnificent kiss.

She ought to have dabbed the moist handkerchief on his lips since the laudanum had obviously left them parched. She meant to ease out of his arms and attend to the task, but he deepened the kiss.

Her body responded like kindling, for his touch, the sensation of his mouth on hers, the slide of his tongue along the seam of her lips, and the arousing weight of his body ignited a fire within her that she had no desire to douse.

She doubted she could, even if she wanted to...which she decidedly did not.

Yet, the proper part of her was telling her to get up off the bed at once before her reputation wound up in tatters. The proper part of her was telling her to remember the reason she'd come in here in the first place.

Retrieve your necklace and leave.

How could she when she was hardly able to move with his big body weighing her down? And what harm could there be? His eyes were glassy, and she suspected that he was sleeping... Perhaps a waking sleep induced by the massive dose of laudanum he'd been given.

His hand drifted up to cup her breast.

Sweet mercy!

Who knew a big, calloused paw could feel so good?

When she made no protest, he began to knead her breast, his touch fiery despite the layers of silk gown and linen corset between them. When she still made no protest – how could she when she'd forgotten how to speak – his touch grew bolder.

Fireworks exploded inside her body as he stroked his thumb across–

She really had to stop him, but... *Oh my.*

More fireworks. He didn't know what he was doing.

Well, he did.

His touch was exquisite.

But he thought he was lost in a dream. Touching her breast in a dream. She ought to... What did she mean to say?

Oh, yes. She ought to stop him. It had been on the tip of her tongue to tell him, but the words simply melted away.

She moaned instead.

She might have uttered, "Don't stop," or perhaps it was "Don't ever stop, you big, handsome Scot," and arched her back to better accommodate the position of his hand to her breast.

No, she couldn't have said something so absurd aloud.

"Ye did, lass." Which explained why he continued to run his thumb over its tautening bud, and then his mouth closed over the hard peak, suckling and nipping through the fabric. *Oh, even sweeter mercy!* She'd have to change out of her gown, of course. She couldn't very well walk down to supper with a stain over her breast, a big, wet circle that looked like the bull's eye on a target.

Silk hid nothing.

The slightest drop of water would cause a stain.

"Loopy, is it really you? It canno' be," Thad said with a raspy groan that tore from the back of his throat. "Ye're so soft and beautiful. My beautiful dream."

His mouth moved to her other breast, his lips closing over the peak of that mound. *Twin targets.* She felt the dampness of his flicking tongue seep through the fabric layers down to her skin.

Oh, goodness.

She meant to stop him. "Don't stop," she whispered instead, and wound her fingers in his hair as he continued to work his magic. Who was more depraved? Him or her? It had to be her, for he was an unconscious beast struggling to wake and believing she was only in his fantasies.

She was a coward who wanted to know his touch, even if it meant making a fool of herself. Even if it meant sinking to this base level.

She knew it was wrong, but never experiencing his touch was unbearable. She wouldn't marry him unless he truly loved her. Laudanum-induced passion did not count. If not drugged, could he ever look at her the way Beast had looked at Olivia? Or the way her brother had looked at Poppy?

She could accept no less from Thad.

His hand trailed lower to find its way under her gown. At the same time, he kissed his way up to the little pulse that was wildly throbbing at the base of her neck. "Ye taste so good, lass, just like a–"

"Don't you dare say it!"

"—sausage patty."

Even when dreaming, he could not stop thinking of food. Couldn't he be a little more romantic? She slid out from under him and stumbled to her feet.

She wanted to leave, but her hair was a mess, half the pins fallen out and probably sticking into the ribs of the big oaf sprawled atop her bed who now appeared to be passed out and snoring again.

Only he wasn't a big oaf.

His touch had felt so good.

His kisses still had her body in a hot tingle.

Penelope stared down at herself and groaned.

She was the oaf and the fool.

Her gown was wet around her breasts, but since it laced up the back, she couldn't reach the ties to undo them. She went to her armoire to grab another gown, perhaps a scarlet one to mark herself as a wanton, because had Thad not bothered to speak and merely concentrated on teasing her body into a passionate frenzy, she would not have stopped him.

Thankfully, his comment had reminded her of what he truly thought of her. A side of pork. And that had tossed ice water on her hot, little body with sufficient force to cool it off.

She stared at the gowns arranged neatly in her armoire and selected a delicate, tea-rose silk. Of course, she had only delicate colors, no vivid scarlets, since she was a sweet, young thing, and the palest hues were all that were deemed proper for sweet innocents to wear for more formal affairs.

She was so busy staring at the gown she'd selected, she did not realize Thad had come up behind her.

"Lass, ye're real," he said in a reverent whisper, stealing his arm around her waist and drawing her up against his overly warm body. Oh, she was going straight to hell. He was running a low fever.

She'd taken advantage of a drugged, sick man.

"Why are ye in here? What happened?"

She set aside the new gown. *Don't be naked. Don't be naked.* And turned to face him.

His eyes widened in surprise, for his gaze had shot to her chest and there was no mistaking what he'd been doing to her to create those stains.

And she'd allowed it.

But her own expression was one of relief, for he'd had the presence of mind to don his breeches.

"Did I do that to ye, lass?" He ignored her shame and distress, casting her a tender grin. Indeed, the fiend was grinning from ear to ear. "No wonder I woke up with a mouthful of lint."

A fiery heat roared into her cheeks.

"I'll help ye into the new frock."

She shoved his hand away. "I don't need your help. You've done quite enough. I'll manage it myself."

"All those laces? And it took two of us to do 'quite enough.' Dinna turn prim on me, lass. *Oooh, Thad. Ye big, sexy, Scottish devil. Don't stop.*" He turned her around so that her back faced him and then he kissed the nape of her neck.

She felt a big ball of humiliation lodge in her chest. "I know. I'm so sorry. It was all my fault. Please don't make fun of me."

"Blessed saints, lass. Is that what ye think I'm doing?" He swallowed her in his arms, drawing her firmly against his chest. "I've dreamed of this moment for months now. How could I possibly dream of anyone else when I've *loved* ye for years?"

"What?"

"Ye heard me, lass. I love ye."

Was this the laudanum speaking? Or did he truly feel this way?

"Thad, I'll forgive you if you remember none of this in the morning. You're drugged. Your mind is hazy."

"It's clearer than it's ever been." He kissed her on the neck again, a perfect kiss with just the right amount of passion and tenderness. "I've felt this way all along. But I never intended to act on it, for ye're an English earl's daughter and I was a cast-off, forgotten lad. The closest thing I had to a mother was toothless, ill-tempered Fiona."

Penelope closed her eyes and stilled against him, soaking in his warmth and the honey richness of his voice.

"Then I met my schoolmate's sister. A little girl with the biggest green eyes and a smart mouth who reminded me of a wild strawberry growing amid the hedgerows. A little girl who showed me the only tenderness I'd ever known." He kissed the top of her head. "That little girl is my heaven, I said to myself. I knew it then and there. When I grow up, I'm going to marry her."

Penelope dared not release the breath she had been holding.

"But as I got older, I realized the impossibility of such a match. A big nobody daring to offer for a little princess?"

"Thad." Tears stung her eyes.

"I'll love ye till the day I die, Loopy. How can anyone else ever claim my heart?"

"Oh, Thad." If only he meant it. But how could she trust his words in this drugged state?

Tears streamed down her cheeks.

He turned her to face him and placed his hands on either side of her face. "No tears, lass." He gently wiped them away with his thumbs.

She closed her eyes and shuddered. "Please don't say anything more. You don't know what you're saying. Don't give me hope today and then crush it tomorrow."

"I won't."

"This is ridiculous. Look at me?" She glanced down at the front of her gown. "And look at you?" His hair was spiked where she'd run her fingers through it to keep his head at her breast. He still looked magnificent.

"Ridiculous," she repeated, for he was not only drugged and feverish, but likely talking in his sleep.

"Aye, lass. We'll never be a staid or proper pair. This is the way it will always be for us. Silly. Ridiculous. Passionate. Imperfect."

"Embarrassing."

"How else can a big, stubborn Scot with enough laudanum in him to fell a horse and a smart-mouthed Sassenach with the most beautiful breasts in all of England ever be? Och, lass. Do ye think I care what anyone thinks? I love ye. All of ye. Yer smart mouth and yer luscious body. Lord, ye have a luscious body. Don't make me shut off my low brain. I canno' do it, not around you."

He meant to kiss her, but a scratch at the door followed by a high-pitched bark caused them to quickly separate.

Penelope rushed to the door. "Periwinkle, what are you doing in the hall?" She lifted him into her arms and laughed when he began to slobber her with licks and kisses.

A minute later, a breathless Emily hurried down the hall toward them. "Oh, m'lady! Thank goodness you've found him. Your aunt was so afraid he'd run out of the house. But look, he's wet the front of your gown. Oh, bad Periwinkle!"

Thad cast her an innocent look.

Penelope cleared her throat. "I merely came in here to fetch a new gown for myself. The tea-rose silk. Let's take it back to Aunt Lavinia's bedchamber. I'll change into it there."

"Aye, m'lady." Emily was too busy taking in Thad's body to think about the gown Penelope was holding out to her.

"Emily, let's leave Laird Caithness." She turned to Thad, trying to maintain a prim expression. "I'm sorry I disturbed your slumber."

He leaned his good shoulder lazily against the door frame and cast her a sleepy, utterly devastating smile. "Ye didn't disturb me, lass. I was dreaming of ye anyway."

Emily erupted in a fit of giggles the moment he shut the door behind them. "Oh, m'lady! Did you hear that naughty man?"

Penelope sighed and hurried down the hall. "I heard him."

"And him wearing only his breeches. Nothing but a few buttons between–"

"Emily!" Penelope stopped to gape at her.

The girl gave a lusty moan. "If that big Scot were dreaming of me, why I'd have my hands on his buttons so quick, he–"

"Enough!" She continued down the hall, now at Lavinia's door.

Emily was still muttering. "If I had an itch, he'd know how to scratch it proper. I'm just saying, m'lady."

"I'm a lady, Emily. I can't have an *itch*." Although there was no other excuse for what she'd allowed Thad to do to her just now. "I'd have to be married to Laird Caithness to allow him to scratch it, wouldn't I?"

Her maid shrugged. "Well, what's to stop you?"

Penelope shook her head. "What?"

"What's to stop you from marrying that big Scot?"

Nothing, she supposed. But what if his admission of love had only been a drug-induced fantasy that he would not remember in the morning?

She would find out tomorrow. Thad was in too much of a stupor to dine with them this evening. Would he wake in time to meet her at the pond after breakfast tomorrow?

Once the drug was out of his system, she doubted she'd get a confession of love out of him.

Would she have the courage to admit she loved him?

CHAPTER THIRTEEN

A LIGHT MIST still lingered over the pond the following morning. Penelope had skipped breakfast and walked down there early, her stomach too tied in knots for her to attempt to eat. She hadn't slept well either, tossing and turning all night. Periwinkle hadn't helped, for the dog continued to show his displeasure of her presence in *his* side of Lavinia's bed.

He'd constantly poked his nose where it didn't belong, sniffing her and then following it up with a snuffle of indignation.

She patted the faded red leather binding of The Book of Love she'd brought along with her. "Does he truly love me?"

She set the book aside on the fallen log and began to stroll along the bank. She'd worn her walking boots and a gown of russet cotton with a shawl of matching swirls of russet and gold. Her hair was loosely plaited in one long braid down her back.

Perhaps she ought to have made herself up more fashionably, but Thad was never one who cared for style, although his casual attire always looked magnificent on him and never out of place, even at the fanciest *ton* gatherings.

With his rugged good looks and commanding aspect, he created a style all his own.

"Loopy, there ye are. I thought ye were still in the house," he called out, striding toward her like a conquering hero, his saddlebag slung over his good shoulder. As expected, he was not properly attired, merely clad in brown breeches and a white lawn shirt, as well as his tall brown boots.

She pursed her lips as her gaze settled on the saddlebag. "Are you going somewhere?"

"No. Just here." He dropped the bag atop the fallen log under the shade tree where she'd earlier set down her book. "Come, lass. Sit beside me and let's talk."

She nodded and settled on the log. "Thad, I'm so sorry for–"

"Hush, lass. I'm not." He sat down beside her. "Ye look beautiful," he said in a husky rumble, tugging lightly on her braid. "I like yer hair down."

She couldn't help but blush. "So do you. Look handsome, that is."

He grinned at her.

And continued to grin at her.

"Why are you looking at me that way?"

He arched an eyebrow. "I canno' stop thinking about what ye let me do to ye, was it only yesterday? I'm still picking lint off my tongue."

Her cheeks caught fire. "Gad, you're impossible."

"Why? I'm speaking the truth. And do ye hear me complaining? No, not in the least." His gaze turned smoldering and his voice husky. "But the next time I touch ye like that, it won't be through layers of clothes. It's the taste of yer sweet skin I'll be wanting to feel on my tongue."

"Thad!"

His eyebrow was still quirked upward in that devilishly appealing way she'd come to know well. "There will be a next time, Loopy. A lifetime, I hope."

She glanced away to stare across the pond. The mist was melting away, and a mother duck and her ducklings were bobbing along the shimmering water. "You said you loved me."

"Aye, lass. I remember. I meant it. I have no intention of taking it back."

She dared herself to turn back to him and look into his eyes, but her cheeks were still on fire and she suddenly felt like the biggest coward ever to exist. "Are you sure, Thad?"

His grin faded. "More certain than I've ever been about anything in my life. This is real, Loopy." He sighed and shook his head. "Och, I suppose I should stop calling ye that. Ye always hated the name."

She placed her hand on his arm as she turned to face him. "It doesn't matter anymore. I don't think I'd respond to Penelope if you ever called me that. In truth, I never minded. I just said I did because you were so irksome at times, and sometimes I merely wished to irk you in return."

"Perhaps a compromise is in order. How about I call ye *mo cridhe?*"

"What does it mean?"

"My love." He turned away and began to rummage through his saddlebag.

"What are you doing?" As her hand slipped off his arm, she placed it over her heart to still its rapid beat. *Mo cridhe.* My love. Was it possible?

"Ye need proof that I'm not lying to ye about my feelings."

"I know you wouldn't lie to me." Her eyes grew wide, for she was startled by the comment. "I trust you."

"Verra well, then ye're afraid I'm lying to myself. Ye think I was dazed and rambling last night. Ye think I told Caithness and Hume I had offered for ye merely to save my own hide." He leaned forward and cast her an achingly tender smile. "It was to save my *heart* not my thick Scottish hide. Ye're the only girl I've ever loved or ever will love, and here's the proof of it."

He dug into his pouch and withdrew a handful of what appeared to be letters. "Every one ye ever wrote me, lass. I have them all right here. I carry them with me always. To the Highlands. Into battle. Here with me now." He handed them to her.

She took them in her shaky fingers. "You kept them?"

"Every last one."

She opened the top letter and chuckled as she read it. It was one of her first to him and she couldn't have been more than eight or nine years old. *"Dear Thaddius, I hope you are well. We missed you at Easter. I wanted to save you a slice of ham, but Nathaniel ate it. I was so angry I kicked him. Father sent me up to my room without supper. I would do it again because I know you like food. Cook says you eat like a wolf starved through winter. Cook sent up some raisin scones for me. I saved them for you instead. Nathaniel promised to give them to you when he returned to school. I hope you like them. Your friend, Penelope Sherbourne (Nathaniel's sister)."*

She folded it and opened another one. *"Dear Thaddius, I hope you are well."* She glanced up at him and laughed softly. "I was rather a dull writer."

He cast her a heartbreakingly tender smile. "No, lass. Ye were perfect."

"Oh, this is another early one." She continued to read. *"Mother says I should not have stolen your clothes. She says I must apologize to you and this time mean it sincerely. I told her you deserved it. She sent me up to my room without supper. Cook sent up some raisin scones for me. I saved them for you instead. Do you still eat like a wolf starved through winter? Your friend, Penelope Sherbourne (Nathaniel's sister)."*

She wiped away a tear that had fallen onto her cheek. "Goodness, I never realized my letters were so silly."

His gaze remained achingly tender. "They weren't silly. They were beautiful."

She opened one of the later letters, one sent to him after he, Nathaniel, and Beast had gone off to war. *"Dear Thaddius, I hope you are well."* She snorted. "Oh, goodness. I am the worst writer in creation!"

"No, ye're not. Read on."

"Olivia, Poppy, and I pray for you every day. We pray for Nathaniel and Beast as well. Father won't talk to me about the war and perhaps it is for the best. He isn't in good health, but we are doing our best to make him comforta-

ble. *Thinking of perils the three of you face daily makes us all very sad. I wish I could do something for you. I don't like being home and unable to do anything to help. So I had Cook teach me how to bake. I taught Poppy and Olivia. The three of us make cakes and biscuits, but I also always make raisin scones for the regiments that pass through Wellesford. Somehow, it brings me closer to you. The soldiers seem to appreciate the gesture. It is such a small thing. I think of you often and worry that you're starving. Please keep yourself safe and come back to us. We are your family (your English family) and we love you as our own. If you are not yet sick of raisin scones, I will bake as many as you like upon your return. But don't tell Father or Aunt Lavinia. They say it isn't seemly for a gently bred young woman to have her hands covered in flour up to her elbows, and that no young man will marry me if he finds out I've been working in the kitchen. I may have responded rudely to the notion. They sent me up to my room without supper. Cook sent up some raisin scones. I wanted to send them to you. I cried because I didn't know where you were or if you were still alive. Please be alive, Thad. I'll lose a big piece of my heart forever if you're not. Your friend, Penelope Sherbourne (Nathaniel's sister)."*

She was crying in earnest now. "I knew you were still alive. I felt it in my heart."

He put his arms around her. "Do you still doubt that I love ye, Loopy? What those letters did for me...to know someone cared. To know *you* cared. I thought of you every day. I looked forward to receiving your letters."

"I wrote like a simpleton. Always mentioning raisin scones, and apparently, I was often sent up to my room without supper. But I continued to sign my letters the way I had when I was a little girl. It was a jest to be shared just between us."

He laughed softly. "I know, and it brought a smile to my lips with each letter, knowing it was something you would do. I wouldn't change who you are. And I like that ye speak yer mind, always blazing yer own trail."

His expression sobered. "I know you always prayed for me, but I did the same for you. Especially at the start of each battle. I didn't know if I would survive, so I worried about who was going to look after ye if I didn't make it back to England. Not that ye really needed looking after. My concern was for yer happiness. Ye deserve to be loved by someone who understands ye and loves ye for yer stubbornness, yer tenderness. Yer passion and yer smart mouth."

He kissed her softly on the mouth. "It's a beautiful mouth."

"Oh, Thad."

"I told myself the first thing I was going to do once the blasted war was over was ride to Sherbourne Manor to taste one of yer raisin scones. I like the scones, of course. But what I really wanted was to see the girl who had written me these letters. I may be a Caithness, and now it seems I'm to be a Hume, but I've always thought of Wellesford as my home because of you."

He leaned forward and kissed her once more. "When I returned a few months ago and saw ye all grown up, my heart soared. I hadn't seen ye in a few years. I thought ye'd turn out pretty, but I wasn't prepared for how beautiful ye'd become. Ye were an angel. Ye stole my breath away then and there. Ye still do."

He glanced at The Book of Love. "The three of ye were so intent on figuring out how to make a man fall in love. *Mo cridhe*, I was already wildly in love with ye. Only I never would have let ye know. Ye deserved someone as grand as Wycke."

"I never cared about rank or title."

"But I did. Oh, not for myself. For you, lass." He shook his head and groaned. "Ironic that Hume, the very man who disowned my mother and never once cared whether I lived or died, should be the one who brought about this miracle for me. I'm his heir. Heir to an earl." He shook his head and laughed. "I was with Hume and Caithness at Castlereagh's home when I first learned of this windfall. All I could think of was you, and how I could now offer for yer hand in marriage with my head held high."

He gathered the letters and tucked them back in his saddlebag, then bent on one knee before Penelope. He took her trembling hand in his. "Let me ask ye proper this time. Will ye marry me?"

She was about to accept him, but her response was interrupted as they both turned toward the house, startled by a sudden commotion. They heard shouts and loud, yipping barks mingled with female cries of alarm. "Oh, Thad! It's Periwinkle. He's run out of the house."

"He's coming this way. I'll get him." He rose to intercept the little spaniel who wasn't much bigger than the average squirrel.

Penelope was up on her feet now. "I'll help."

But Periwinkle had other plans. He darted past both of them and leaped into the pond to chase the ducks who were paddling in the water. They quacked in panic and disappeared into the rushes. At the same moment, Periwinkle realized he was in deep water and did not know how to swim.

Apparently, he did not realize dogs were supposed to know how to paddle with their paws. "Oh, Thad. He's going under!"

Penelope jumped into the water, her heart leaping frantically as his little head disappeared below the surface.

"Loopy, no! Yer gown!"

As it began to tangle in her legs, she realized she couldn't kick herself upward, not only because of the tangled fabric, but from the weight of her gown that was also tugging her downward. She felt herself sinking, and felt a growing sense of alarm as she held her breath and followed Periwinkle in disappearing beneath the surface.

But she managed to grab hold of the frightened dog and was about to push him toward the shore and worry about breathing afterward, when she felt herself suddenly lifted upward.

She took a deep, gasping breath the moment her head broke above the surface.

Thad had her.

She clutched his big body, held on tight as with two quick strokes, he swam them all to shore beside the copse of trees. She wanted to thank him and tell him that she loved him, but was coughing too hard to speak.

Periwinkle began to bark and squirm in her arms. He was unharmed and back to his demanding self, but she dared not let him go.

When she blinked open her eyes, she saw Nathaniel and Pip running toward them. In the next moment, Nathaniel took the wayward dog into his arms. "Nice work, Loopy. I'll take him back to the house. Lavinia's still shrieking. Poppy's trying to calm her."

Penelope hadn't found her voice yet, so she merely nodded.

"Are ye all right, lass?" Thad asked once Nathaniel and Pip had left them to return to the house. He still held her in his arms and was stroking her wet hair. All of her was soaked. So was he, and he looked magnificent.

She nodded.

Oh, how she wanted to tell him that she loved him!

She tried, but got no more out than "Thad" before she coughed again.

But he had to know, for his gaze turned tender and his smile reached all the way into his eyes. "Lass, ye're wet again."

She laughed. "And we're in the copse again." Her voice was raspy, but it was clearing.

His gaze remained on her. "Och, ye gave me a scare."

Now groaning and laughing, he swallowed her in his embrace. Then he was kissing her on the mouth, on her forehead. On her closed eyes. On her mouth again in a long and lingering kiss that curled her toes and had her clutching the front of his wet shirt. "Will ye marry me, Penelope?"

She loved him, too. In truth, it scared her how much she loved him.

Those letters.

So silly, and yet he'd treasured them.

"Yes, I'll marry you. I love you, Thad. To the depths of my soul."

CHAPTER FOURTEEN

L OOPY WAS SMILING at him as they made their way back to the house. Thad had the letters safely tucked back in his leather pouch that was tossed over his good shoulder. The beauty beside him had The Book of Love tucked under her arm.

"What do ye think, lass? Will we surprise everyone? Or will we get a hearty round of *we knew it all along?*"

She shook her head and laughed, holding the book up to him. "This will now take on mythical proportions. Olivia won her duke. Poppy won her earl. And I won the best of all, a Highlander."

He took her hand in his as they continued walking. "Your big, dumb Scot."

She groaned. "Thad, no. The man of my dreams. You've always been that, only I was too scared to admit it because I didn't think you liked me."

He entwined his fingers in hers and gave them a light squeeze. "We were as wrong about each other as two people can possibly be." He glanced at the book and grinned. "I think we're going to have to *listen* to each other better. Stop working at cross purposes."

"Where's the fun in that?"

He tossed back his head and laughed. "Right, lass. No fun at all. I rather liked that love-crazed Harpy who somehow fell into my arms yesterday."

"Thad," she said quietly, now serious, "Speaking of that...I know we'll bicker from time to time."

He snorted.

"But I don't ever want us to go to bed angry with each other."

"Och, Loopy. I'm a simple, low-brained male. Once ye're in my bed, I won't be thinking of the fight we had that day. I won't be thinking, period. I'll be taking ye into my arms and hoping ye'll allow me to explore that sweet body of yours." He paused in his stride as they neared the entry to the manor house. "If I could marry ye today, I would."

She nodded. "I suppose there's the business end to take care of now that you've become an important person."

"Yer brother's going to enjoy negotiating the betrothal contract. I'm sure Beast will join in that discussion. They'll have great sport at my expense. Hume and Caithness will sit in as well to make certain I don't give away my entire inheritance."

"No chance of that. My brother can't wait to be rid of me. I think he'd pay you a king's ransom to take me off his hands." She furrowed her brow and began to nibble her lip. "Thad, I'll have to speak to Lord Wycke. I think it's only fair that I tell him before we spread the news to our friends and family. He'll be disappointed, but I don't think he'll be terribly hurt."

"Aye, lass. Do ye want me to tell him with ye?"

"No, that would only be rubbing salt in the wound. Although he won't really be distressed. Nor is he likely to do anything mad, such as attempt to abduct me." She looked up into his eyes as though searching for something in his expression. "What would you have done if the situation had been reversed and I'd chosen Wycke?"

"Nothing, lass, if I thought ye loved him. But anything short of love?" He arched an eyebrow and grinned. "I would have ridden into the church on Thor, swept ye up in my arms, and galloped off with ye. But it would not have come to that. Ye've too much passion in ye to marry for anything less than love."

"Passion? That's a nice way of describing my nature. My brother thinks I'm obstinate and impossibly thickheaded."

"Ye are that, too. We've already agreed upon that. But so am I. Our coupling will be no tame affair. I doubt the bed will remain in one piece by the time we're through."

She blushed fiercely, her innocence surging to the fore. It amazed him that she could be so spirited and brash, yet so shy in this way. He liked this about her. "I'm jesting, lass. Ye need have no fear of our wedding night. Ye're no mere *vessel into which I'll spill my seed.* If ye don't want me to touch ye, I won't."

They were standing together, soaking wet. She looked so achingly beautiful, he couldn't bear it. Little beads of water still dripped from her hair onto her cheeks and down her neck. Her gown, now ruined, was pasted to her luscious body, outlining every curve. Indeed, he'd better get her upstairs before the men in the house, from footmen to earls, got too close a look. "Ye'd better change out of that gown before ye go talking to anybody."

She nodded. "I will. In truth, I'm shivering. Autumn is upon us and the water was cold."

He glanced at the tell-tale signs on her breasts, for he was a shameless hound and couldn't stop gawking.

But he was cold and wet, too. On the outside, at least. Inside, he was in flames over this girl. That she had accepted his proposal, that she loved him…he could not begin to explain what he felt. Someone was obviously smiling down on him from heaven.

He turned her over to her maid and then went in search of Nathaniel.

He ran into Poppy and Goose first. "Lavinia has finally calmed down," Poppy assured him. "Thank you for rescuing Periwinkle."

He nodded. "Loopy saved him." Then he'd had to save her, but it wasn't worth mentioning.

Goose chuckled. "Whoever would have thought it of that pampered pup? I'm sorry I missed all the excitement. Beast and I ought to have walked over earlier." She studied Thad. "You jumped in, too. Something more than a mere rescue must have happened. You look different, somehow. What changed, Thad?" Suddenly, she gasped. "You're in love!"

Poppy's big blue eyes widened to saucers. "I knew it! You had to fall in love. You were Penelope's test frog!"

He wasn't going to admit he'd loved her all his life. "Where's Nathaniel?"

"In his study with Beast," Goose said. "Where's Penelope?"

"Upstairs, changing into a dry gown."

They abandoned him to race upstairs. So much for secrets or for letting Wycke know before they broke the news to everyone. He didn't mind so much. Those three lasses practically shared one heart. Whatever one felt, the other two always seemed to sense.

He supposed it was similar for Beast, Nathaniel, and him. Not blood kin, but brothers bound forever in their hearts. He walked into Nathaniel's study, for the door was ajar and his friends were casually seated across from each other. But they rose when he stepped in and closed the door behind him.

He tried not to drip too badly on Nathaniel's expensive carpet. "Nathaniel…"

"Blister it, Thad," he said, eyeing him from head to toe, and then chuckling. "You too?"

Beast burst out laughing. "The Book of Love will now become legend. Our wives will have to keep it under lock and key. Or bury it somewhere deep in the ground, else it will be stolen."

Thad nodded. "They're upstairs together right now, probably discussing who to give it to next. But I can't pity the man who'll be the next test frog. There's nothing wrong with marrying for love."

Nathaniel ran a hand raggedly through his hair. "So, you're sure about this?"

Thad nodded again. "I loved yer sister from the first moment I saw her. Obviously, a pure, childhood love back then. The miracle wasn't ever in making me fall in love with her. I always have and always will. But I had nothing to offer her until a few weeks ago. Now I'm Hume's heir." He glanced up toward the ceiling. "A gift from heaven? Or was it the book that brought this about?"

Nathaniel crossed his arms over his chest and cast him a gloating smile. "You do realize I'm going to roll right over you in the betrothal negotiations. Can you stop mooning over my sister long enough to make this something of a battle?"

"Och, no. I dinna think I can."

"THEN WE'RE AGREED," Penelope whispered later that morning when Poppy and Olivia joined her along the parade route. "Violet's next?"

The pair nodded.

"Thank you," Poppy said, giving each of them a quick hug. "I want my sister to experience the same happiness as we share with our husbands. Or soon to be husband for you, Penelope. I must admit, Thad's the smartest out of the three of them. Olivia and I had to beat Nathaniel and Beast about the head with that book before anything penetrated their thick skulls."

"Thad loved you in silence all along." Olivia sighed. "That's so romantic."

Her big Scot romantic?

Not so much in words, but certainly in deeds.

Her heart fluttered as she noticed Thad and Pip striding to the outskirts of town, both of them wearing slings on their arm. Pip was gazing up at Thad in adoration, for Thad had insisted Pip march beside him since they were family now. Those slings were almost an afterthought, for neither of them appeared to be in pain despite the freshness of their injuries.

She supposed happiness had a way of dulling one's pain.

Penelope and her friends shared a secret smile when Violet joined them. "Don't they all look wonderful?" Violet squealed. "I'm sorry Anne and her family could not stay a day longer. Anne was sorely disappointed. So was Malcolm. You should have seen the kiss he gave her as she was about to climb into her carriage. Practically sucked the lips off her. Lord Wycke was furious. But his mother did not appear to be very much overset. She merely told her son to stop being a stubborn dolt and allow them to move up their wedding date."

Penelope was relieved when her friends changed the topic of conversation. In truth, telling Anne's brother she loved Thad and had agreed to marry him, had disappointed Wycke more than she'd expected. The man had never shown much feeling when in her company, but she supposed Thad hadn't either, and he'd been deeply in love with her.

Perhaps she'd have a talk with Wycke when they met again, for they were certain to see each other on occasion now that Thad's cousin was going to marry Wycke's sister. If Wycke thought his sister's romance would come to a natural end, he was sorely mistaken.

Penelope understood these Highlanders better now.

They were stubborn.

They knew what they wanted and would not be dissuaded by reason.

Malcolm MacLauren was going to marry Anne Halford, and that was that.

She returned her attention to the parade since it was about to start.

Thad's regiment had already gathered at the edge of Wellesford, the men clad in their Caithness clan tartans. The war was over for these men. They'd been proud to be a part of the Scots Greys, but their hearts would always be in Caithness. They'd put aside their uniforms for this day and donned their kilts.

She had to admit, Thad looked devastatingly handsome in a rugged, brawny way.

A distant keen of bagpipes and the steady beat of a drum signaled the regiment was on the march. Miss Billings darted across the street to join them. "Goodness, what excitement. I do love my books, but this parade is so much better."

Indeed, every merchant had closed up shop and turned out for this event. To Penelope's surprise, she noticed Poppy move closer to Miss Billings and put her arm in hers. It was a small gesture, but obviously not to Miss Billings who responded with a smile so bright, she shone like a diamond.

And Poppy thought she'd never make a proper countess?

Goodness, Penelope had been raised to assume this role and did not do it half so well as Poppy who'd had no training, but understood the demands of the role instinctively.

She tucked this bit of knowledge away, knowing it would be put to good use when she and Thad arrived at Coldstream Castle, the Earl of Hume's seat. The Hume clan would have to be won over, for they'd regard her and Thad as outsiders, even if he was his grandfather's heir. She could be as stubborn and determined as any Scot. The way to win them over would not be by exerting one's authority. It would be done over time by gaining their friendship and respect.

She supposed Thad knew this, for her big Scot was not in the least slow-witted.

Shaking out of her thoughts, she cheered as the soldiers marched past. Pip was in the vanguard along with Thad, his giant cousins, and the two Scottish earls.

But the parade stalled when Thad suddenly broke ranks and strode toward her. "Thad?" She eyed him warily. "What are you doing?"

The citizens of Wellesford seemed to understand his purpose better than she did. They began to whoop and holler when he drew her into his one good arm and crushed his mouth to hers to give her a kiss that – in Violet's earlier words – practically sucked the lips off her.

Oh, heavens!

She couldn't wait to get this man into her bed. Lord forgive her for the wicked thought, but she really, desperately wanted this man in her bed.

"I love ye, Loopy."

"Likewise, you big oaf."

Which he took as permission to kiss her again. "Och, ye taste delicious. Just like–"

"Don't say it!"

"—a sausage patty."

CHAPTER FIFTEEN

Wellesford, England
November 1815

T HERE WAS NOTHING more beautiful than the crisp, vibrant blue of a cloudless November sky, Penelope decided while taking an early morning stroll to the pond. A flock of geese had taken it over this morning, no doubt using this little patch of water as a rest stop. She had no idea where they were going, but she'd seen hundreds of them flying southward.

She tucked her shawl more securely about her shoulders, for the wind had picked up and there was a chill to it.

"Ye're up early, *mo cridhe*," Thad said, coming up beside her. He'd returned to Sherbourne Manor yesterday with his two uncles, Caithness and Hume, and his cousins, Robbie and Malcolm. He'd also brought along a special license.

They would marry within a few hours.

She'd known this day was in the offing and was quite ready for it.

She, Poppy, and Olivia had prepared, sending invitations to the townspeople and the local gentry. Cook and her kitchen staff had been cooking and baking all week. The maids and footmen had spent these past days dusting, polishing, and moving furniture aside to make room for the crowd of well-wishers soon to gather at Sherbourne Manor for the wedding breakfast.

"I know this day will be difficult for ye, lass." He drew her up against his chest so that they both faced outward, toward the pond. "I hope ye'll come to love our new home as much as ye love this place."

She nodded. "I will, Thad. I'll be happy wherever you are. This is Poppy and Nathaniel's home now. I'll enjoy visiting here, but we'll make our own memories elsewhere." She turned in his arms to face him.

He had a wicked gleam in his eyes.

She groaned. "Why are you looking at me that way?"

"It's early. No one is awake yet." He gazed toward the copse of trees. "Ye've seen me naked there. I've seen ye almost naked there. The geese are flying off now, leaving the pond just to ourselves."

"Are you suggesting we go for a swim?" She gasped. "The water's freezing."

"Nowhere near freezing, lass. Just a little on the cool side. Our Highland summers are much like this and our lochs never get above this temperature. I'll warm ye up if ye get cold. What do ye say?"

She laughed and shook her head. "You are mad."

He lifted her into his arms, his shoulder nicely healed and showing no signs of stiffness or pain. "Aye, driven mad with desire for ye." He carried her into the grove of trees and the shelter of the underbrush, wasting not a moment before he began to undress.

"You're serious? You're going in the water?"

He nodded. "Care to join me?"

She sighed. "I must be mad as well." She removed her shawl and set it aside on a nearby branch that was now almost bare of its leaves.

Fortunately, there were enough pines and rushes, and late blooming foliage on the surrounding trees to give them cover. "Aren't we supposed to become responsible adults now that we'll soon be wed?"

He shrugged. "What does yer precious book say about it?"

He was referring to The Book of Love, of course. "I'm sure it says nothing about this. Or if it does, it advises not to do anything idiotic the morning of your wedding." They would be married within a few hours and share a cozy bedchamber from this evening on. They'd have plenty of opportunities to do all manner of things not deemed proper.

"But ye're marrying a big, dumb Scot." His gaze was boyish and wicked and so filled with love, she simply could not resist him.

"A big, wonderful Scot," she corrected with a groan of surrender. She and Thad did not seem to do anything the proper way. Why start now? "And you are about to marry a love-crazed Harpy. Are you sure we're only going to swim?"

"I can be talked into doing more."

His hands were now sliding up and down her body, turning her blood to liquid pools of fire. She had no intention of stopping him, for she was experiencing new and wondrous sensations in response to his touch and would not be averse to allowing something more than a dip in the water.

She arched an eyebrow. "Your low brain hard at work, is it?"

"Aye. Always with ye, lass."

Against her better judgement, she helped him off with his shirt. In typical Thad fashion, he'd dressed casually, wearing buff pants and a shirt. Not even a gentleman's shirt, but one more suited to a farmer about to plow a field. No buttons or studs. This allowed the garment to be easily drawn over his head, displaying his massive, rippling muscles.

And oh, did this man have a fine body.

"Thad," she said with a sudden ache to her voice.

He caressed her cheek. "I feel it too, lass."

She supposed she ought to have insisted they wait until this evening. But when had she and Thad ever done anything according to Society's rules? It seemed right that they should ignore the rules now. In truth, she liked that they misbehaved. More important, she wanted Thad to know that she loved him now and always.

Her love for him existed beyond the bond of marriage.

She trusted him with her heart.

She knew it was precious to him and he would protect her from harm until his last, gasping breath, and never cause her any hurt.

Perhaps they would take greater care to behave themselves once they had children, if they were so blessed. "Thad, about that something more. I can be talked into it, too."

"Are ye sure, lass?"

She nodded.

"Blessed saints, what a relief." He wasted no time in unfastening the laces of her gown and drawing the fashionably styled bodice down to her waist. She had no time to feel the bite of the chill wind, for his lips and hands were all over her, touching, exploring, *tasting* her. Sweet heaven! What this man did to her.

She laughed as he nibbled along the curve of her neck, for he had yet to shave and the bristle forming along his jaw tickled her. But her light laughter quickly turned to moans of delight as her body warmed and her senses heightened in response to his touch.

He slid his arm around her waist, drawing her close as her legs turned to butter and she feared they would never hold her up.

She also dared to explore him, reaching up on tiptoes to kiss him on the mouth, enjoying the warm press of his lips against hers when he responded to her touch. She trailed kisses along his broad shoulders and the curve of his neck, feeling the heat of his skin against her mouth and tasting its salty tang on her tongue.

"Lass, I wish to taste ye, too." She inhaled sharply as he cupped her breast and began to knead it gently. He swirled his tongue lazily across its straining tip. Then his mouth was on her breast, suckling and nipping and stealing her breath away with the wonder of it.

She thought she might expire, for her heart was now beating so fast, she could not slow it down, nor did she care to slow this mounting, frenzied pleasure. Lost in the moment, she failed to realize her gown had slipped off her body until she almost tripped over it as it lay pooled at her feet. Oh, heavens! Were all innocents this clumsy? "I'm so sorry. I…"

"Och, love." He bent to set aside her gown. As he rose, he removed her chemise for unhampered access to her body.

His look of wonder caused any shame she was feeling to melt away. Her hair was unbound and she was going to use the tumbling cascade to cover herself, but stopped.

This man.

What he did to her with his caresses and the smoldering heat of his desire.

She felt a pulsing warmth build between her legs as he continued to touch her and explore. This was her body craving his, no doubt. She'd never experienced such longing, nor had she ever felt such aching emptiness inside of her. It was a good ache, a desire to take Thad into her body. An ache that only he could satisfy.

She whispered his name and clutched his shoulders because she couldn't bear to let him go.

"I've got you, my love." He lowered his mouth to her breast once again, his tongue flicking over its swollen tip and drawing a moan of pleasure from her lips. At the same time, he slid his hand to the V of her legs and cupped her there, holding still for a long moment to allow her to absorb the intimacy of his hand upon her. "It wasn't my intention to rush ye. I'll wait, if ye wish."

"No, Thad. Heavens, my heart is about to burst."

He laughed softly. "So is mine."

She held on to him, gripping the hard, golden muscles of his arms as he began to stroke her intimately. She sensed his tension, for he was holding back his own hot need, his only thought to pleasure her. He was a magnificent beast, this big, rugged Scot who had stolen her heart. "I love you, Thad."

He set her down on his shirt that was spread out over the carpet of fallen leaves. *"Mo cridhe,"* he whispered, removing his fingers where he'd stroked her and replacing them with – oh, sweet mercy! – with his mouth. "Thad!"

"Let me taste ye, lass." He dipped his head to her most intimate spot, his mouth now on her and touching her with his lips and tongue as he'd done to her breasts. Only this was...they were in danger of setting the copse ablaze with the scorching heat of their desire.

Her blood turned thick and molten.

Her skin was aflame.

This feeling was something raw and savage and eternal. She'd only read about the senses, but now she understood their power with every thrum and throb of her body. Nothing would satisfy her but to take this man inside her.

Yet, as she tugged on his shoulders to bring him up to her, she felt a tingling heat rush through her and an inexplicable lightness surround her. She was being carried to a place she'd never been before.

A place where she *felt* everything.

She clutched the edges of his shirt, as though the coarse fabric was enough to prevent her from floating away. But she needn't have worried, Thad's hands were on her, caressing her. Holding her to him so that she would not be lost in the air.

When it seemed she could bear no more, the world suddenly erupted before her eyes. The scent of pine and impending winter surrounded her as she took deep, gasping breaths. Thad replaced his mouth with his finger and shifted his hard, muscled body upward to rest on his elbows and watch her as her body soared to new and unexplored heights. "*Mo cridhe*, let yerself go."

She did, because she couldn't stop the sensations rushing through her. When she soared, he was there to catch her as she slowly floated down to earth.

He swallowed her in his arms to warm her damp, trembling body. Wordlessly, he held her against his chest, caressing her. Running his fingers gently through her hair.

She felt the wild beat of his heart against her own.

And felt his hard, aching need pressed against her thigh.

She would have allowed him his release and was surprised that he did not take advantage. Instead, he carried her into the water and swam with her in his arms. "We both need to cool off, lass."

"I thought you'd…"

"I'll claim ye tonight, my love. When I have the husbandly right to do so. But I wanted this moment for us. I wanted to taste ye. To breathe ye in and know yer scent in the mindless, low-brain way a beast would know its mate. Our connection runs deeper than shared memories or mere attraction. It extends beyond our bodies. It's in our souls."

The water was cold, but Penelope only felt the warmth of the moment.

Thad held her in his powerful arms.

This man loved her.

He kissed her again and then began to swim them back to shore, for the household would soon awaken, and they were both without their clothes.

"Oh, my heavens!" Her eyes grew wide as a sudden, distressing thought gripped her.

"What's wrong, lass?"

"Do you think Pip's awake?"

Thad groaned. "Bollocks, I hope not."

They returned to the copse in haste, seeking their garments. "Thank The Graces, the lad hasn't touched them," Thad muttered, picking up his shirt and using it to dry her off. "Ye're so beautiful, lass. I dinna think I can keep my hands off ye until this evening."

She turned to pick up her chemise and slip it over her head, her body still thrumming and her blood still coursing hotly through her veins despite the dip in the cold water. "Oh, Thad. What we did just now…" She blushed furiously. "I had no idea loving someone could ever be like this."

"Ye felt so good in my arms, lass. It'll be even better tonight, although I expect I'll make a fool of myself. I won't be able to hold back, ye give me that much pleasure." He lazily rubbed his shirt against his golden skin.

Penelope's heart melted. "Help me on with my gown. I'm scheduled to marry a big, handsome Scot this morning, and I have no wish to be late."

"Nor does he." He put on his pants, then helped her on with her gown, which turned into a most inefficient affair because they were distracted kissing each other. But Thad allowed nothing more than kisses. "Tonight, lass." He glanced skyward. "Lord, help me survive until then."

He took her hand in his as they walked back to the house together.

Since his shirt was wet, he did not bother to put it on, but merely draped it over his shoulder.

When they entered the house, he turned her over to her waiting maid and left to ready himself for their wedding which would take place shortly. "Lud, m'lady," Emily said, licking her lips as Thad walked off. "I hope that he made love to you proper. Now, don't you go blushing and pretending nothing happened. I can tell by the heat in your cheeks and the fire in his eyes that something did. Well, I always said that big Scot would know how to do it proper."

THAD TOOK EVERYONE'S ribbing in good nature. Nothing was going to dampen his enjoyment of this perfect day. Loopy now stood before him, looking like a blessed angel in a gown of cream silk and lace. There might have been pearls sewn in as well. He wasn't really looking at her gown, but recalling the exquisitely soft body hidden beneath it.

Vicar Carstairs cleared his throat. "Thaddius MacLauren, Laird

Caithness, Captain…" he began to recite his military honors and a list of titles recently bestowed on him now that he was Hume's heir. "Do you take…" The 'aye' was ready to spring from his lips, but he waited until the vicar had finished reciting Penelope's name and string of her connections.

"I do," he said with a nod, taking Penelope's hand and giving it a light squeeze.

Penelope responded with a solemn "I do" to the vicar's question similarly posed to her. But he knew by the way her fingers entwined in his, that she was ready to leap out of her skin with excitement. However, she held herself together like a proper lady, obviously trained in the genteel arts and knowing how to use them when necessary.

Never with him, however.

Lord, he couldn't wait to be alone with the wild Penelope, the beautiful girl who'd clutched the edges of his shirt and allowed herself to soar under the guidance of his touch. *Tonight. And ever after.* He only had a few more hours to get past before he held her in his arms again.

And he was counting the minutes.

They left the church and rode through Wellesford, taking a turn through the town before heading to Sherbourne Manor where the wedding breakfast would be held. "You look handsome in your uniform," Loopy said, smiling up at him as they rode in her brother's open curricle, the better to be seen by those who had turned out for the wedding.

"Ye look lovely in yer gown." He grinned. "Ye'll look lovelier without it, but that'll have to wait, I suppose."

She rolled her eyes. "Yes, it will have to wait. Besides, you must be hungry by now."

He shrugged. "I'm always hungry, lass. Verra well, I'll wait until after we've eaten to carry ye away. Not that we've far to go. Or that we'll have much privacy since we're staying here for the night." He sighed. "Nor will we have much privacy at Coldstream Castle, but at least there, we'll have our own private quarters. It's a big, rambling fortress. Built and rebuilt many times over."

"I'll make do. I don't care where we are so long as we're together."

He nodded. "I have a bride gift for ye, lass."

She tipped her head to smile at him. "Dare I ask what it is?"

"Malcolm and Robbie said I was an idiot. But I had the jeweler fashion it anyway." He fished into his pocket and withdrew a tiny box. "It's a charm, to be worn on a bracelet or a necklace."

She opened the box and stared at the gift, obviously puzzled by what it was. In the next moment, she understood and gasped. "Thad, it's a raisin scone!"

"The raisins are tiny sapphires. The scone is silver."

Tears formed in her eyes. "Are ye crying, lass?"

She nodded. "This is the best gift ever."

He sighed in relief. "Aye, I knew ye'd understand and appreciate my meaning. It isn't just a charm ye'll be wearing, it's my heart. It's all of me. My every hope. My every dream. My every wish come true."

"I know, Thad. I appreciate it more than I can say."

But that night, as the festivities ended and everyone retired to their quarters, she showed him just how much she did appreciate him. He was afraid he might hurt her when they coupled, for he was that eager to fulfill their union. But she was ready for him, her body warm and her arms inviting as they opened to him.

After he'd brought her to passion and claimed his own, he took her into his arms and held her close against his body. "I love ye, lass."

"How much do you love me?"

"Och, dinna ask such a question."

Was he supposed to say something romantic, perhaps something poetic? But only one thing came to mind, and he knew she wouldn't like it. She stared at him, giving him *that look*, and he knew he had to give her an answer. She'd understood the meaning in the charm he'd given her earlier today. He hoped she would understand his response to her question, for one thing had always stood out for him when reading The Book of Love. The chapters dealt with sensations, the power of the five senses. His sense had always been taste.

A hunger for the love he'd been deprived of as a child.

A hunger for food, because he was a big ox even as a boy and didn't get that way by being shy around food.

A hunger for Penelope because no one and nothing tasted sweeter than this girl.

Indeed, his was the sense of taste.

No one satisfied it better than Penelope. "How much do I love ye? I love ye more than a sausage patty."

There, he'd said it.

He braced himself, prepared to be kicked out of bed.

Instead, she snuggled closer. "Thank you, Thad. I'm flattered."

"Ye are?" Indeed, this angel understood him.

"Yes, my love." She leaned her body over his and gave him a kiss on the lips.

He loved the way her auburn hair spilled over her bare shoulders and onto his chest. He loved the feel of her soft lips against his mouth. And the softness of her body as she rested it against him. All of her was soft and beautiful. Soft and warm and pink. "How much do ye love me?"

"That's easy, Thad." She lay atop him now, her breasts pillowed against his chest. "I love you to the depths of my soul."

He rolled her under him, shifting their positions in one swift move. "Och, lass. That's a good answer. Much better than mine."

She cupped his face in her hands. "Yours was perfect. It was *you*. Will you make love to me a second time?"

"I'm at yer service, lass. As many times as ye wish."

Book of Love Series

Book 1 – The Look of Love

Book 2 – The Touch of Love

Book 3 – The Taste of Love

Also by Meara Platt

FARTHINGALE SERIES
My Fair Lily
The Duke I'm Going To Marry
Rules For Reforming A Rake
A Midsummer's Kiss
The Viscount's Rose
Earl Of Hearts
If You Wished For Me
Never Dare A Duke
Capturing The Heart Of A Cameron

THE BOOK OF LOVE SERIES
The Look of Love
The Touch of Love
The Taste of Love

De WOLFE "ANGELS" SERIES
Nobody's Angel
Kiss An Angel
Bhrodi's Angel

DARK GARDENS SERIES
Garden of Shadows
Garden of Light
Garden of Dragons
Garden of Destiny

THE BRAYDENS
A Match Made In Duty
Earl of Westcliff
Fortune's Dragon

PIRATES OF BRITANNIA
Pearls of Fire

About the Author

Meara Platt is a USA Today bestselling author and an award winning, Amazon UK All-star. Her favorite place in all the world is England's Lake District, which may not come as a surprise since many of her stories are set in that idyllic landscape, including her Romance Writers of America Golden Heart award winning story released as Book 3 in her paranormal romance Dark Gardens series. If you'd like to learn more about the ancient Fae prophecy that is about to unfold in the Dark Gardens series, as well as Meara's lighthearted, international bestselling Regency romances in the Farthingale Series, please visit Meara's website at www.mearaplatt.com.

Website:

www.mearaplatt.com

CPSIA information can be obtained
at www.ICGtesting.com
Printed in the USA
LVHW010936230821
695886LV00002B/224